Against Nature

Against Nature

by Joris-Karl Huysmans

Wilder Publications, LLC.
PO Box 243
Blacksburg, VA 24060

ISBN 10: 1-60459-671-6
ISBN 13: 978-1-60459-671-7

Table of Contents

Chapter 1. 6

Chapter 2. 13

Chapter 3. 19

Chapter 4. 26

Chapter 5. 37

Chapter 6. 45

Chapter 7. 58

Chapter 8. 68

Chapter 9. 78

Chapter 10. 86

Chapter 11. 96

Chapter 12. 108

Chapter 13. 127

Chapter 14. 137

Chapter 15. 157

Chapter 16. 166

Chapter 1

The Floressas Des Esseintes, to judge by the various portraits preserved in the Château de Lourps, had originally been a family of stalwart troopers and stern cavalry men. Closely arrayed, side by side, in the old frames which their broad shoulders filled, they startled one with the fixed gaze of their eyes, their fierce moustaches and the chests whose deep curves filled the enormous shells of their cuirasses.

These were the ancestors. There were no portraits of their descendants and a wide breach existed in the series of the faces of this race. Only one painting served as a link to connect the past and present—a crafty, mysterious head with haggard and gaunt features, cheekbones punctuated with a comma of paint, the hair overspread with pearls, a painted neck rising stiffly from the fluted ruff.

In this representation of one of the most intimate friends of the Duc d'Epernon and the Marquis d'O, the ravages of a sluggish and impoverished constitution were already noticeable.

It was obvious that the decadence of this family had followed an unvarying course. The effemination of the males had continued with quickened tempo. As if to conclude the work of long years, the Des Esseintes had intermarried for two centuries, using up, in such consanguineous unions, such strength as remained.

There was only one living scion of this family which had once been so numerous that it had occupied all the territories of the Ile-de-France and La Brie. The Duc Jean was a slender, nervous young man of thirty, with hollow cheeks, cold, steel-blue eyes, a straight, thin nose and delicate hands.

By a singular, atavistic reversion, the last descendant resembled the old grandsire, from whom he had inherited the pointed, remarkably fair beard and an ambiguous expression, at once weary and cunning.

His childhood had been an unhappy one. Menaced with scrofula and afflicted with relentless fevers, he yet succeeded in crossing the breakers of adolescence, thanks to fresh air and careful attention. He grew stronger, overcame the languors of chlorosis and reached his full development.

His mother, a tall, pale, taciturn woman, died of anæmia, and his father of some uncertain malady. Des Esseintes was then seventeen years of age.

He retained but a vague memory of his parents and felt neither affection nor gratitude for them. He hardly knew his father, who usually resided in Paris. He recalled his mother as she lay motionless in a dim room of the Château de Lourps. The husband and wife would meet on rare occasions, and he remembered those lifeless interviews when his parents sat face to face in front of a round table faintly lit by a lamp with a wide, low-hanging shade, for the duchesse could not endure light or sound without being seized with a fit of nervousness. A few, halting words would be exchanged between them in the gloom and then the indifferent duc would depart to meet the first train back to Paris.

Jean's life at the Jesuit school, where he was sent to study, was more pleasant. At first the Fathers pampered the lad whose intelligence astonished them. But despite their efforts, they could not induce him to concentrate on studies requiring discipline. He nibbled at various books and was precociously brilliant in Latin. On the contrary, he was absolutely incapable of construing two Greek words, showed no aptitude for living languages and promptly proved himself a dunce when obliged to master the elements of the sciences.

His family gave him little heed. Sometimes his father visited him at school. "How are you . . . be good . . . study hard . . . "—and he was gone. The lad passed the summer vacations at the Château de Lourps, but his presence could not seduce his mother from her reveries. She scarcely noticed him; when she did, her gaze would rest on him for a moment with a sad smile—and that was all. The moment after she would again become absorbed in the artificial night with which the heavily curtained windows enshrouded the room.

The servants were old and dull. Left to himself, the boy delved into books on rainy days and roamed about the countryside on pleasant afternoons.

It was his supreme delight to wander down the little valley to Jutigny, a village planted at the foot of the hills, a tiny heap of cottages capped with thatch strewn with tufts of sengreen and clumps of moss. In the open fields, under the shadow of high ricks, he would lie, listening to the hollow splashing of the mills and inhaling the fresh breeze from Voulzie. Sometimes he went as far as the peat-bogs, to the green and black hamlet of Longueville, or climbed wind-swept hillsides affording magnificent views. There, below to one side, as far as the eye could reach, lay the Seine valley, blending in the distance with the blue sky; high up, near the horizon, on the other side, rose the churches and tower of Provins which seemed to tremble in the golden dust of the air.

Immersed in solitude, he would dream or read far into the night. By protracted contemplation of the same thoughts, his mind grew sharp, his vague, undeveloped ideas took on form. After each vacation, Jean returned to his masters more reflective and headstrong. These changes did not escape them. Subtle and observant, accustomed by their profession to plumb souls to their depths, they were fully aware of his unresponsiveness to their teachings. They knew that this student would never contribute to the glory of their order, and as his family was rich and apparently careless of his future, they soon renounced the idea of having him take up any of the professions their school offered. Although he willingly discussed with them those theological doctrines which intrigued his fancy by their subtleties and hair-splittings, they did not even think of training him for the religious orders, since, in spite of their efforts, his faith remained languid. As a last resort, through prudence and fear of the harm he might effect, they permitted him to pursue whatever studies pleased him and to neglect the others, being loath to antagonize this bold and independent spirit by the quibblings of the lay school assistants.

Thus he lived in perfect contentment, scarcely feeling the parental yoke of the priests. He continued his Latin and French studies when the whim seized him and, although theology did not figure in his schedule, he finished his apprenticeship in this science, begun at the

Château de Lourps, in the library bequeathed by his grand-uncle, Dom Prosper, the old prior of the regular canons of Saint-Ruf.

But soon the time came when he must quit the Jesuit institution. He attained his majority and became master of his fortune. The Comte de Montchevrel, his cousin and guardian, placed in his hands the title to his wealth. There was no intimacy between them, for there was no possible point of contact between these two men, the one young, the other old. Impelled by curiosity, idleness or politeness, Des Esseintes sometimes visited the Montchevrel family and spent some dull evenings in their Rue de la Chaise mansion where the ladies, old as antiquity itself, would gossip of quarterings of the noble arms, heraldic moons and anachronistic ceremonies.

The men, gathered around whist tables, proved even more shallow and insignificant than the dowagers; these descendants of ancient, courageous knights, these last branches of feudal races, appeared to Des Esseintes as catarrhal, crazy, old men repeating inanities and time-worn phrases. A fleur de lis seemed the sole imprint on the soft pap of their brains.

The youth felt an unutterable pity for these mummies buried in their elaborate hypogeums of wainscoting and grotto work, for these tedious triflers whose eyes were forever turned towards a hazy Canaan, an imaginary Palestine.

After a few visits with such relatives, he resolved never again to set foot in their homes, regardless of invitations or reproaches.

Then he began to seek out the young men of his own age and set.

One group, educated like himself in religious institutions, preserved the special marks of this training. They attended religious services, received the sacrament on Easter, frequented the Catholic circles and concealed as criminal their amorous escapades. For the most part, they were unintelligent, acquiescent fops, stupid bores who had tried the patience of their professors. Yet these professors were pleased to have bestowed such docile, pious creatures upon society.

The other group, educated in the state colleges or in the lycées, were less hypocritical and much more courageous, but they were neither more interesting nor less bigoted. Gay young men dazzled by operettas and races, they played lansquenet and baccarat, staked large fortunes on horses and cards, and cultivated all the pleasures enchanting to brainless fools. After a year's experience, Des Esseintes felt an overpowering weariness of this company whose debaucheries seemed to him so unrefined, facile and indiscriminate without any ardent reactions or excitement of nerves and blood.

He gradually forsook them to make the acquaintance of literary men, in whom he thought he might find more interest and feel more at ease. This, too, proved disappointing; he was revolted by their rancorous and petty judgments, their conversation as obvious as a church door, their dreary discussions in which they judged the value of a book by the number of editions it had passed and by the profits acquired. At the same time, he noticed that the free thinkers, the doctrinaires of the bourgeoisie, people who claimed every liberty that they might stifle the opinions of others, were greedy and shameless puritans whom, in education, he esteemed inferior to the corner shoemaker.

His contempt for humanity deepened. He reached the conclusion that the world, for the most part, was composed of scoundrels and imbeciles. Certainly, he could not hope to discover in others aspirations and aversions similar to his own, could not expect companionship with an intelligence exulting in a studious decrepitude, nor anticipate meeting a mind as keen as his among the writers and scholars.

Irritated, ill at ease and offended by the poverty of ideas given and received, he became like those people described by Nicole—those who are always melancholy. He would fly into a rage when he read the patriotic and social balderdash retailed daily in the newspapers, and would exaggerate the significance of the plaudits which a sovereign public always reserves for works deficient in ideas and style.

Already, he was dreaming of a refined solitude, a comfortable desert, a motionless ark in which to seek refuge from the unending deluge of human stupidity.

A single passion, woman, might have curbed his contempt, but that, too, had palled on him. He had taken to carnal repasts with the eagerness of a crotchety man affected with a depraved appetite and given to sudden hungers, whose taste is quickly dulled and surfeited. Associating with country squires, he had taken part in their lavish suppers where, at dessert, tipsy women would unfasten their clothing and strike their heads against the tables; he had haunted the green rooms, loved actresses and singers, endured, in addition to the natural stupidity he had come to expect of women, the maddening vanity of female strolling players. Finally, satiated and weary of this monotonous extravagance and the sameness of their caresses, he had plunged into the foul depths, hoping by the contrast of squalid misery to revive his desires and stimulate his deadened senses.

Whatever he attempted proved vain; an unconquerable ennui oppressed him. Yet he persisted in his excesses and returned to the perilous embraces of accomplished mistresses. But his health failed, his nervous system collapsed, the back of his neck grew sensitive, his hand, still firm when it seized a heavy object, trembled when it held a tiny glass.

The physicians whom he consulted frightened him. It was high time to check his excesses and renounce those pursuits which were dissipating his reserve of strength! For a while he was at peace, but his brain soon became over-excited. Like those young girls who, in the grip of puberty, crave coarse and vile foods, he dreamed of and practiced perverse loves and pleasures. This was the end! As though satisfied with having exhausted everything, as though completely surrendering to fatigue, his senses fell into a lethargy and impotence threatened him.

He recovered, but he was lonely, tired, sobered, imploring an end to his life which the cowardice of his flesh prevented him from consummating.

Once more he was toying with the idea of becoming a recluse, of living in some hushed retreat where the turmoil of life would be muffled—as in those streets covered with straw to prevent any sound from reaching invalids.

It was time to make up his mind. The condition of his finances terrified him. He had spent, in acts of folly and in drinking bouts, the greater part of his patrimony, and the remainder, invested in land, produced a ridiculously small income.

He decided to sell the Château de Lourps, which he no longer visited and where he left no memory or regret behind. He liquidated his other holdings, bought government bonds and in this way drew an annual interest of fifty thousand francs; in addition, he reserved a sum of money which he meant to use in buying and furnishing the house where he proposed to enjoy a perfect repose.

Exploring the suburbs of the capital, he found a place for sale at the top of Fontenay-aux-Roses, in a secluded section near the fort, far from any neighbors. His dream was realized! In this country place so little violated by Parisians, he could be certain of seclusion. The difficulty of reaching the place, due to an unreliable railroad passing by at the end of the town, and to the little street cars which came and went at irregular intervals, reassured him. He could picture himself alone on the bluff, sufficiently far away to prevent the Parisian throngs from reaching him, and yet near enough to the capital to confirm him in his solitude. And he felt that in not entirely closing the way, there was a chance that he would not be assailed by a wish to return to society, seeing that it is only the impossible, the unachievable that arouses desire.

He put masons to work on the house he had acquired. Then, one day, informing no one of his plans, he quickly disposed of his old furniture, dismissed his servants, and left without giving the concierge any address.

Chapter 2

More than two months passed before Des Esseintes could bury himself in the silent repose of his Fontenay abode. He was obliged to go to Paris again, to comb the city in his search for the things he wanted to buy.

What care he took, what meditations he surrendered himself to, before turning over his house to the upholsterers!

He had long been a connoisseur in the sincerities and evasions of color-tones. In the days when he had entertained women at his home, he had created a boudoir where, amid daintily carved furniture of pale, Japanese camphor-wood, under a sort of pavillion of Indian rose-tinted satin, the flesh would color delicately in the borrowed lights of the silken hangings.

This room, each of whose sides was lined with mirrors that echoed each other all along the walls, reflecting, as far as the eye could reach, whole series of rose boudoirs, had been celebrated among the women who loved to immerse their nudity in this bath of warm carnation, made fragrant with the odor of mint emanating from the exotic wood of the furniture.

Aside from the sensual delights for which he had designed this chamber, this painted atmosphere which gave new color to faces grown dull and withered by the use of ceruse and by nights of dissipation, there were other, more personal and perverse pleasures which he enjoyed in these languorous surroundings,—pleasures which in some way stimulated memories of his past pains and dead ennuis.

As a souvenir of the hated days of his childhood, he had suspended from the ceiling a small silver-wired cage where a captive cricket sang as if in the ashes of the chimneys of the Château de Lourps. Listening to the sound he had so often heard before, he lived over again the silent evenings spent near his mother, the wretchedness of his suffering, repressed youth. And then, while he yielded to the voluptuousness of the woman he mechanically caressed, whose words or laughter tore him from his revery and rudely recalled him to the moment, to the boudoir, to reality, a tumult arose in his soul, a need of avenging the sad years he had endured, a mad wish to sully the recollections of his family by shameful action, a furious desire to pant on cushions of flesh, to drain to their last dregs the most violent of carnal vices.

On rainy autumnal days when melancholy oppressed him, when a hatred of his home, the muddy yellow skies, the macadam clouds assailed him, he took refuge in this retreat, set the cage lightly in motion and watched it endlessly reflected in the play of the mirrors, until it seemed to his dazed eyes that the cage no longer stirred, but that the boudoir reeled and turned, filling the house with a rose-colored waltz.

In the days when he had deemed it necessary to affect singularity, Des Esseintes had designed marvelously strange furnishings, dividing his salon into a series of alcoves hung with varied tapestries to relate by a subtle analogy, by a vague harmony of joyous or sombre, delicate or barbaric colors to the character of the Latin or French books he loved. And he would seclude himself in turn in the particular recess whose décor seemed best to correspond with the very essence of the work his caprice of the moment induced him to read.

He had constructed, too, a lofty high room intended for the reception of his tradesmen. Here they were ushered in and seated alongside each other in church pews, while from a pulpit he preached to them a sermon on dandyism, adjuring his bootmakers and tailors implicitly to obey his briefs in the matter of style, threatening them with pecuniary excommunication if they failed to follow to the letter the instructions contained in his monitories and bulls.

He acquired the reputation of an eccentric, which he enhanced by wearing costumes of white velvet, and gold-embroidered waistcoats, by inserting, in place of a cravat, a Parma bouquet in the opening of his shirt, by giving famous dinners to men of letters, one of which, a revival of the eighteenth century, celebrating the most futile of his misadventures, was a funeral repast.

In the dining room, hung in black and opening on the transformed garden with its ash-powdered walks, its little pool now bordered with basalt and filled with ink, its clumps of cypresses and pines, the dinner had been served on a table draped in black, adorned with baskets of violets and scabiouses, lit by candelabra from which green flames blazed, and by chandeliers from which wax tapers flared.

To the sound of funeral marches played by a concealed orchestra, nude negresses, wearing slippers and stockings of silver cloth with patterns of tears, served the guests.

Out of black-edged plates they had drunk turtle soup and eaten Russian rye bread, ripe Turkish olives, caviar, smoked Frankfort black pudding, game with sauces that were the color of licorice and blacking, truffle gravy, chocolate cream, puddings, nectarines, grape preserves, mulberries and black-heart cherries; they had sipped, out of dark glasses, wines from Limagne, Roussillon, Tenedos, Val de Penas and Porto, and after the coffee and walnut brandy had partaken of kvas and porter and stout.

The farewell dinner to a temporarily dead virility—this was what he had written on invitation cards designed like bereavement notices.

But he was done with those extravagances in which he had once gloried. Today, he was filled with a contempt for those juvenile displays, the singular apparel, the appointments of his bizarre chambers. He contented himself with planning, for his own pleasure, and no longer for the astonishment of others, an interior that should be comfortable although embellished in a rare style; with building a curious, calm retreat to serve the needs of his future solitude.

When the Fontenay house was in readiness, fitted up by an architect according to his plans, when all that remained was to determine the color scheme, he again devoted himself to long speculations.

He desired colors whose expressiveness would be displayed in the artificial light of lamps. To him it mattered not at all if they were lifeless or crude in daylight, for it was at night that he lived, feeling more completely alone then, feeling that only under the protective covering of darkness did the mind grow really animated and active. He also experienced a peculiar pleasure in being in a richly illuminated room, the only patch of light amid the shadow-haunted, sleeping houses. This was a form of enjoyment in which perhaps entered an element of vanity, that peculiar pleasure known to late workers when, drawing aside the window curtains, they perceive that everything about them is extinguished, silent, dead.

Slowly, one by one, he selected the colors.

Blue inclines to a false green by candle light: if it is dark, like cobalt or indigo, it turns black; if it is bright, it turns grey; if it is soft, like turquoise, it grows feeble and faded.

There could be no question of making it the dominant note of a room unless it were blended with some other color.

Iron grey always frowns and is heavy; pearl grey loses its blue and changes to a muddy white; brown is lifeless and cold; as for deep green, such as emperor or myrtle, it has the same properties as blue and merges into black. There remained, then, the paler greens, such as peacock, cinnabar or lacquer, but the light banishes their blues and brings out their yellows in tones that have a false and undecided quality.

No need to waste thought on the salmon, the maize and rose colors whose feminine associations oppose all ideas of isolation! No need to consider the violet which is completely neutralized at night; only the red in it holds its ground—and what a red! a viscous red like the lees of wine. Besides, it seemed useless to employ this color, for by using a certain amount of santonin, he could get an effect of violet on his hangings.

These colors disposed of, only three remained: red, orange, yellow.

Of these, he preferred orange, thus by his own example confirming the truth of a theory which he declared had almost mathematical correctness—the theory that a harmony exists between the sensual nature of a truly artistic individual and the color which most vividly impresses him.

Disregarding entirely the generality of men whose gross retinas are capable of perceiving neither the cadence peculiar to each color nor the mysterious charm of their nuances of light and shade; ignoring the bourgeoisie, whose eyes are insensible to the pomp and splendor of strong, vibrant tones; and devoting himself only to people with sensitive pupils, refined by literature and art, he was convinced that the eyes of those among them who dream of the ideal and demand illusions are generally caressed by blue and its derivatives, mauve, lilac and pearl grey, provided always that these colors remain soft and do not overstep the bounds where they lose their personalities by being transformed into pure violets and frank greys.

Those persons, on the contrary, who are energetic and incisive, the plethoric, red-blooded, strong males who fling themselves unthinkingly into the affair of the moment, generally delight in the bold gleams of yellows and reds, the clashing cymbals of vermilions and chromes that blind and intoxicate them.

But the eyes of enfeebled and nervous persons whose sensual appetites crave highly seasoned foods, the eyes of hectic and over-excited creatures have a predilection toward that irritating and morbid color with its fictitious splendors, its acid fevers—orange.

Thus, there could be no question about Des Esseintes' choice, but unquestionable difficulties still arose. If red and yellow are heightened by light, the same does not always hold true of their compound, orange, which often seems to ignite and turns to nasturtium, to a flaming red.

He studied all their nuances by candlelight, discovering a shade which, it seemed to him, would not lose its dominant tone, but would stand every test required of it. These preliminaries completed, he sought to refrain from using, for his study at least, oriental stuffs and rugs which have become cheapened and ordinary, now that rich merchants can easily pick them up at auctions and shops.

He finally decided to bind his walls, like books, with coarse-grained morocco, with Cape skin, polished by strong steel plates under a powerful press.

When the wainscoting was finished, he had the moulding and high plinths painted in indigo, a lacquered indigo like that which coachmakers employ for carriage panels. The ceiling, slightly rounded, was also lined with morocco. In the center was a wide opening resembling an immense bull's eye encased in orange skin—a circle of the firmament worked out on a background of king blue silk on which were woven silver seraphim with out-stretched wings. This material had long before been embroidered by the Cologne guild of weavers for an old cope.

The setting was complete. At night the room subsided into a restful, soothing harmony. The wainscoting preserved its blue which seemed sustained and warmed by the orange. And the orange remained pure, strengthened and fanned as it was by the insistent breath of the blues.

Des Esseintes was not deeply concerned about the furniture itself. The only luxuries in the room were books and rare flowers. He limited himself to these things, intending later on to hang a few drawings or paintings on the panels which remained bare; to place shelves and book racks of ebony around the walls; to spread the pelts of wild beasts and the skins of blue fox on the floor; to install, near a massive fifteenth century counting-table, deep armchairs and an old chapel reading-desk of forged iron, one of those old lecterns on which the deacon formerly placed the antiphonary and which now supported one of the heavy folios of Du Cange's Glossarium mediae et infimae latinitatis.

The windows whose blue fissured panes, stippled with fragments of gold-edged bottles, intercepted the view of the country and only permitted a faint light to enter, were draped with curtains cut from old stoles of dark and reddish gold neutralized by an almost dead russet woven in the pattern.

The mantel shelf was sumptuously draped with the remnant of a Florentine dalmatica. Between two gilded copper monstrances of Byzantine style, originally brought from the old Abbaye-au-Bois de Bièvre, stood a marvelous church canon divided into three separate compartments delicately wrought like lace work. It contained, under its glass frame, three works of Baudelaire copied on real vellum, with wonderful missal letters and splendid coloring: to the right and left, the sonnets bearing the titles of La Mort des Amants and L'Ennemi; in the center, the prose poem entitled, Anywhere Out of the World—n'importe ou, hors du monde.

Chapter 3

After selling his effects, Des Esseintes retained the two old domestics who had tended his mother and filled the offices of steward and house porter at the Château de Lourps, which had remained deserted and uninhabited until its disposal.

These servants he brought to Fontenay. They were accustomed to the regular life of hospital attendants hourly serving the patients their stipulated food and drink, to the rigid silence of cloistral monks who live behind barred doors and windows, having no communication with the outside world.

The man was assigned the task of keeping the house in order and of procuring provisions, the woman that of preparing the food. He surrendered the second story to them, forced them to wear heavy felt coverings over their shoes, put sound mufflers along the well-oiled doors and covered their floor with heavy rugs so that he would never hear their footsteps overhead.

He devised an elaborate signal code of bells whereby his wants were made known. He pointed out the exact spot on his bureau where they were to place the account book each month while he slept. In short, matters were arranged in such wise that he would not be obliged to see or to converse with them very often.

Nevertheless, since the woman had occasion to walk past the house so as to reach the woodshed, he wished to make sure that her shadow, as she passed his windows, would not offend him. He had designed for her a costume of Flemish silk with a white bonnet and large, black, lowered hood, such as is still worn by the nuns of Ghent. The shadow of this headdress, in the twilight, gave him the sensation of being in a cloister, brought back memories of silent, holy villages, dead quarters enclosed and buried in some quiet corner of a bustling town.

The hours of eating were also regulated. His instructions in this regard were short and explicit, for the weakened state of his stomach no longer permitted him to absorb heavy or varied foods.

In winter, at five o'clock in the afternoon, when the day was drawing to a close, he breakfasted on two boiled eggs, toast and tea. At eleven o'clock he dined. During the night he drank coffee, and sometimes tea and wine, and at five o'clock in the morning, before retiring, he supped again lightly.

His meals, which were planned and ordered once for all at the beginning of each season, were served him on a table in the middle of a small room separated from his study by a padded corridor, hermetically sealed so as to permit neither sound nor odor to filter into either of the two rooms it joined.

With its vaulted ceiling fitted with beams in a half circle, its bulkheads and floor of pine, and the little window in the wainscoting that looked like a porthole, the dining room resembled the cabin of a ship.

Like those Japanese boxes which fit into each other, this room was inserted in a larger apartment—the real dining room constructed by the architect.

It was pierced by two windows. One of them was invisible, hidden by a partition which could, however, be lowered by a spring so as to permit fresh air to circulate around this pinewood box and to penetrate into it. The other was visible, placed directly opposite the porthole built in the wainscoting, but it was blocked up. For a long aquarium occupied the entire space between the porthole and the genuine window placed in the outer wall. Thus the light, in order to brighten the room, traversed the window, whose panes had been replaced by a plate glass, the water, and, lastly, the window of the porthole.

In autumn, at sunset, when the steam rose from the samovar on the table, the water of the aquarium, wan and glassy all during the morning, reddened like blazing gleams of embers and lapped restlessly against the light-colored wood.

Sometimes, when it chanced that Des Esseintes was awake in the afternoon, he operated the stops of the pipes and conduits which emptied the aquarium, replacing it with pure water. Into this, he poured drops of colored liquids that made it green or brackish, opaline or silvery—tones similar to those of rivers which reflect the color of the sky, the intensity of the sun, the menace of rain—which reflect, in a word, the state of the season and atmosphere.

When he did this, he imagined himself on a brig, between decks, and curiously he contemplated the marvelous, mechanical fish, wound like clocks, which passed before the porthole or clung to the artificial sea-weed. While he inhaled the odor of tar, introduced into the room shortly before his arrival, he examined colored engravings, hung on the walls, which represented, just as at Lloyd's office and the steamship agencies, steamers bound for Valparaiso and La Platte, and looked at framed pictures on which were inscribed the itineraries of the Royal Mail Steam Packet, the Lopez and the Valery Companies, the freight and port calls of the Atlantic mail boats.

If he tired of consulting these guides, he could rest his eyes by gazing at the chronometers and sea compasses, the sextants, field glasses and cards strewn on a table on which stood a single volume, bound in sealskin. The book was "The Adventures of Arthur Gordon Pym", specially printed for him on laid paper, each sheet carefully selected, with a sea-gull watermark.

Or, he could look at fishing rods, tan-colored nets, rolls of russet sail, a tiny, black-painted cork anchor—all thrown in a heap near the door communicating with the kitchen by a passage furnished with cappadine silk which reabsorbed, just as in the corridor which connected the dining room with his study, every odor and sound.

Thus, without stirring, he enjoyed the rapid motions of a long sea voyage. The pleasure of travel, which only exists as a matter of fact in retrospect and seldom in the present, at the instant when it is being experienced, he could fully relish at his ease, without the necessity of fatigue or confusion, here in this cabin whose studied disorder, whose transitory appearance and whose seemingly temporary furnishings corresponded so well with the briefness of the time he spent there on his meals, and contrasted so perfectly with his study, a well-arranged, well-furnished room where everything betokened a retired, orderly existence.

Movement, after all, seemed futile to him. He felt that imagination could easily be substituted for the vulgar realities of things. It was possible, in his opinion, to gratify the most extravagant, absurd desires by a subtle subterfuge, by a slight modification of the object of one's wishes. Every epicure nowadays enjoys, in restaurants celebrated for the excellence of their cellars, wines of capital taste manufactured from inferior brands treated by Pasteur's method. For they have the same aroma, the same color, the same bouquet as the rare wines of which they are an imitation, and consequently the pleasure experienced in sipping them is identical. The originals, moreover, are usually unprocurable, for love or money.

Transposing this insidious deviation, this adroit deceit into the realm of the intellect, there was not the shadow of a doubt that fanciful delights resembling the true in every detail, could be enjoyed. One could revel, for instance, in long explorations while near one's own fireside, stimulating the restive or sluggish mind, if need be, by reading some suggestive narrative of travel in distant lands. One could enjoy the beneficent results of a sea bath, too, even in Paris. All that is necessary is to visit the Vigier baths situated in a boat on the Seine, far from the shore.

There, the illusion of the sea is undeniable, imperious, positive. It is achieved by salting the water of the bath; by mixing, according to the Codex formula, sulphate of soda, hydrochlorate of magnesia and lime; by extracting from a box, carefully closed by means of a screw, a ball of thread or a very small piece of cable which had been specially procured from one of those great rope-making establishments whose vast warehouses and basements are heavy with odors of the sea and the port; by inhaling these perfumes held by the ball or the cable end; by consulting an exact photograph of the casino; by eagerly reading the Joanne guide describing the beauties of the seashore where one would wish to be; by being rocked on the waves, made by the eddy of fly boats lapping against the pontoon of baths; by listening to the plaint of the wind under the arches, or to the hollow murmur of the omnibuses passing above on the Port Royal, two steps away.

The secret lies in knowing how to proceed, how to concentrate deeply enough to produce the hallucination and succeed in substituting the dream reality for the reality itself.

Artifice, besides, seemed to Des Esseintes the final distinctive mark of man's genius.

Nature had had her day, as he put it. By the disgusting sameness of her landscapes and skies, she had once for all wearied the considerate patience of æsthetes. Really, what dullness! the dullness of the specialist confined to his narrow work. What manners! the manners of the tradesman offering one particular ware to the exclusion of all others. What a monotonous storehouse of fields and trees! What a banal agency of mountains and seas!

There is not one of her inventions, no matter how subtle or imposing it may be, which human genius cannot create; no Fontainebleau forest, no moonlight which a scenic setting flooded with electricity cannot produce; no waterfall which hydraulics cannot imitate to perfection; no rock which pasteboard cannot be made to resemble; no flower which taffetas and delicately painted papers cannot simulate.

There can be no doubt about it: this eternal, driveling, old woman is no longer admired by true artists, and the moment has come to replace her by artifice.

Closely observe that work of hers which is considered the most exquisite, that creation of hers whose beauty is everywhere conceded the most perfect and original—woman. Has not man made, for his own use, an animated and artificial being which easily equals woman, from the point of view of plastic beauty? Is there a woman, whose form is more dazzling, more splendid than the two locomotives that pass over the Northern Railroad lines?

One, the Crampton, is an adorable, shrill-voiced blonde, a trim, gilded blonde, with a large, fragile body imprisoned in a glittering corset of copper, and having the long, sinewy lines of a cat. Her extraordinary grace is frightening, as, with the sweat of her hot sides rising upwards and her steel muscles stiffening, she puts in motion the immense rose-window of her fine wheels and darts forward, mettlesome, along rapids and floods.

The other, the Engerth, is a nobly proportioned dusky brunette emitting raucous, muffled cries. Her heavy loins are strangled in a cast-iron breast-plate. A monstrous beast with a disheveled mane of black smoke and with six low, coupled wheels! What irresistible power she has when, causing the earth to tremble, she slowly and heavily drags the unwieldy queue of her merchandise!

Unquestionably, there is not one among the frail blondes and majestic brunettes of the flesh that can vie with their delicate grace and terrific strength.

Such were Des Esseintes' reflections when the breeze brought him the faint whistle of the toy railroad winding playfully, like a spinning top, between Paris and Sceaux. His house was situated at a twenty minutes' walk from the Fontenay station, but the height on which it was perched, its isolation, made it immune to the clatter of the noisy rabble which the vicinity of a railway station invariably attracts on a Sunday.

As for the village itself, he hardly knew it. One night he had gazed through his window at the silent landscape which slowly unfolded, as it dipped to the foot of a slope, on whose summit the batteries of the Verrières woods were trained.

In the darkness, to left and right, these masses, dim and confused, rose tier on tier, dominated far off by other batteries and forts whose high embankments seemed, in the moonlight, bathed in silver against the sombre sky.

Where the plain did not fall under the shadow of the hills, it seemed powdered with starch and smeared with white cold cream. In the warm air that fanned the faded grasses and exhaled a spicy perfume, the trees, chalky white under the moon, shook their pale leaves, and seemed to divide their trunks, whose shadows formed bars of black on the plaster-like ground where pebbles scintillated like glittering plates.

Because of its enameled look and its artificial air, the landscape did not displease Des Esseintes. But since that afternoon spent at Fontenay in search of a house, he had never ventured along its roads in daylight. The verdure of this region inspired him with no interest whatever, for it did not have the delicate and doleful charm of the sickly and pathetic vegetation which forces its way painfully through the rubbish heaps of the mounds which had once served as the ramparts of Paris. That day, in the village, he had perceived corpulent, bewhiskered bourgeois citizens and moustached uniformed men with heads of magistrates and soldiers, which they held as stiffly as monstrances in churches. And ever since that encounter, his detestation of the human face had been augmented.

During the last month of his stay in Paris, when he was weary of everything, afflicted with hypochondria, the prey of melancholia, when his nerves had become so sensitive that the sight of an unpleasant object or person impressed itself deeply on his brain—so deeply that several days were required before the impression could be effaced—the touch of a human body brushing against him in the street had been an excruciating agony.

The very sight of certain faces made him suffer. He considered the crabbed expressions of some, insulting. He felt a desire to slap the fellow who walked, eyes closed, with such a learned air; the one who minced along, smiling at his image in the window panes; and the one who seemed stimulated by a whole world of thought while devouring, with contracted brow, the tedious contents of a newspaper.

Such an inveterate stupidity, such a scorn for literature and art, such a hatred for all the ideas he worshipped, were implanted and anchored in these merchant minds, exclusively preoccupied with the business of swindling and money-making, and accessible only to ideas of politics—that base distraction of mediocrities—that he returned enraged to his home and locked himself in with his books.

He hated the new generation with all the energy in him. They were frightful clodhoppers who seemed to find it necessary to talk and laugh boisterously in restaurants and cafés. They jostled you on sidewalks without begging pardon. They pushed the wheels of their perambulators against your legs, without even apologizing.

Chapter 4

A portion of the shelves which lined the walls of his orange and blue study was devoted exclusively to those Latin works assigned to the generic period of "The Decadence" by those whose minds have absorbed the deplorable teachings of the Sorbonne.

The Latin written in that era which professors still persist in calling the Great Age, hardly stimulated Des Esseintes. With its carefully premeditated style, its sameness, its stripping of supple syntax, its poverty of color and nuance, this language, pruned of all the rugged and often rich expressions of the preceding ages, was confined to the enunciation of the majestic banalities, the empty commonplaces tiresomely reiterated by the rhetoricians and poets; but it betrayed such a lack of curiosity and such a humdrum tediousness, such a drabness, feebleness and jaded solemnity that to find its equal, it was necessary, in linguistic studies, to go to the French style of the period of Louis XIV.

The gentle Vergil, whom instructors call the Mantuan swan, perhaps because he was not born in that city, he considered one of the most terrible pedants ever produced by antiquity. Des Esseintes was exasperated by his immaculate and bedizened shepherds, his Orpheus whom he compares to a weeping nightingale, his Aristaeus who simpers about bees, his Aeneas, that weak-willed, irresolute person who walks with wooden gestures through the length of the poem. Des Esseintes would gladly have accepted the tedious nonsense which those marionettes exchange with each other off-stage; or even the poet's impudent borrowings from Homer, Theocritus, Ennius and Lucretius; the plain theft, revealed to us by Macrobius, of the second song of the Aeneid, copied almost word for word from one of Pisander's poems; in fine, all the unutterable emptiness of this heap of verses. The thing he could not forgive, however, and which infuriated him most, was the workmanship of the hexameters, beating like empty tin cans and extending their syllabic quantities measured according to the unchanging rule of a pedantic and dull prosody. He disliked the texture of those stiff verses, in their official garb, their abject reverence for grammar, their mechanical division by imperturbable cæsuras, always plugged at the end in the same way by the impact of a dactyl against a spondee.

Borrowed from the perfected forge of Catullus, this unvarying versification, lacking imagination, lacking pity, padded with useless words and refuse, with pegs of identical and anticipated assonances, this ceaseless wretchedness of Homeric epithet which designates nothing whatever and permits nothing to be seen, all this impoverished vocabulary of muffled, lifeless tones bored him beyond measure.

It is no more than just to add that, if his admiration for Vergil was quite restrained, and his attraction for Ovid's lucid outpourings even more circumspect, there was no limit to his disgust at the elephantine graces of Horace, at the prattle of this hopeless lout who smirkingly utters the broad, crude jests of an old clown.

Neither was he pleased, in prose, with the verbosities, the redundant metaphors, the ludicrous digressions of Cicero. There was nothing to beguile him in the boasting of his apostrophes, in the flow of his patriotic nonsense, in the emphasis of his harangues, in the ponderousness of his style, fleshy but ropy and lacking in marrow and bone, in the insupportable dross of his long adverbs with which he introduces phrases, in the unalterable formula of his adipose periods badly sewed together with the thread of conjunctions and, finally, in his wearisome habits of tautology. Nor was his enthusiasm wakened for Cæsar, celebrated for his laconic style. Here, on the contrary, was disclosed a surprising aridity, a sterility of recollection, an incredibly undue constipation.

He found pasture neither among them nor among those writers who are peculiarly the delight of the spuriously literate: Sallust, who is less colorless than the others; sentimental and pompous Titus Livius; turgid and lurid Seneca; watery and larval Suetonius; Tacitus who, in his studied conciseness, is the keenest, most wiry and muscular of them all. In poetry, he was untouched by Juvenal, despite some roughshod verses, and by Persius, despite his mysterious insinuations. In neglecting Tibullus and Propertius, Quintilian and the Plinies, Statius, Martial, even Terence and Plautus whose jargon full of neologisms, compound words and diminutives, could please him, but whose low comedy and gross humor he loathed, Des Esseintes only began to be interested in the Latin language with Lucan. Here it was liberated, already more expressive and less dull. This careful armor, these verses plated with enamel and studded with jewels, captivated him, but the exclusive preoccupation with form, the sonorities of tone, the clangor of metals, did not entirely conceal from him the emptiness of the thought, the turgidity of those blisters which emboss the skin of the Pharsale.

Petronius was the author whom he truly loved and who caused him forever to abandon the sonorous ingenuities of Lucan, for he was a keen observer, a delicate analyst, a marvelous painter. Tranquilly, without prejudice or hate, he described Rome's daily life, recounting the customs of his epoch in the sprightly little chapters of the Satyricon.

Observing the facts of life, stating them in clear, definite form, he revealed the petty existence of the people, their happenings, their bestialities, their passions.

One glimpses the inspector of furnished lodgings who has inquired after the newly arrived travellers; bawdy houses where men prowl around nude women, while through the half-open doors of the rooms couples can be seen in dalliance; the society of the time, in villas of an insolent luxury, a revel of richness and magnificence, or in the poor quarters with their rumpled, bug-ridden folding-beds; impure sharpers, like Ascylte and Eumolpe in search of a rich windfall; old incubi with tucked-up dresses and plastered cheeks of white lead and red acacia; plump, curled, depraved little girls of sixteen; women who are the prey of hysterical attacks; hunters of heritages offering their sons and daughters to debauched testators. All pass across the pages. They debate in the streets, rub elbows in the baths, beat each other unmercifully as in a pantomime.

And all this recounted in a style of strange freshness and precise color, drawing from all dialects, borrowing expressions from all the languages that were drifting into Rome, extending all the limits, removing all the handicaps of the so-called Great Age. He made each person speak his own idiom: the uneducated freedmen, the vulgar Latin argot of the streets; the strangers, their barbarous patois, the corrupt speech of the African, Syrian and Greek; imbecile pedants, like the Agamemnon of the book, a rhetoric of artificial words. These people are depicted with swift strokes, wallowing around tables, exchanging stupid, drunken speech, uttering senile maxims and inept proverbs.

This realistic novel, this slice of Roman life, without any preoccupation, whatever one may say of it, with reform and satire, without the need of any studied end, or of morality; this story without intrigue or action, portraying the adventures of evil persons, analyzing with a calm finesse the joys and sorrows of these lovers and couples, depicting life in a splendidly wrought language without surrendering himself to any commentary, without approving or cursing the acts and thoughts of his characters, the vices of a decrepit civilization, of an empire that cracks, struck Des Esseintes. In the keenness of the observation, in the firmness of the method, he found singular comparisons, curious analogies with the few modern French novels he could endure.

Certainly, he bitterly regretted the Eustion and the Albutiae, those two works by Petronius mentioned by Planciade Fulgence which are forever lost. But the bibliophile in him consoled the student, when he touched with worshipful hands the superb edition of the Satyricon which he possessed, the octavo bearing the date 1585 and the name of J. Dousa of Leyden.

Leaving Petronius, his Latin collection entered into the second century of the Christian era, passed over Fronto, the declaimer, with his antiquated terms; skipped the Attic Nights of Aulus Gellius, his disciple and friend,—a clever, ferreting mind, but a writer entangled in a glutinous vase; and halted at Apuleius, of whose works he owned the first edition printed at Rome in 1469.

This African delighted him. The Latin language was at its richest in the Metamorphoses; it contained ooze and rubbish-strewn water rushing from all the provinces, and the refuse mingled and was confused in a bizarre, exotic, almost new color. Mannerisms, new details of Latin society found themselves shaped into neologisms specially created for the needs of conversation, in a Roman corner of

Africa. He was amused by the southern exuberance and joviality of a doubtlessly corpulent man. He seemed a salacious, gay crony compared with the Christian apologists who lived in the same century—the soporific Minucius Felix, a pseudo-classicist, pouring forth the still thick emulsions of Cicero into his Octavius; nay, even Tertullian—whom he perhaps preserved for his Aldine edition, more than for the work itself.

Although he was sufficiently versed in theology, the disputes of the Montanists against the Catholic Church, the polemics against the gnostics, left him cold. Despite Tertullian's curious, concise style full of ambiguous terms, resting on participles, clashing with oppositions, bristling with puns and witticisms, dappled with vocables culled from the juridical science and the language of the Fathers of the Greek Church, he now hardly ever opened the Apologetica and the Treatise on Patience. At the most, he read several pages of De culta feminarum, where Tertullian counsels women not to bedeck themselves with jewels and precious stuffs, forbidding them the use of cosmetics, because these attempt to correct and improve nature.

These ideas, diametrically opposed to his own, made him smile. Then the rôle played by Tertullian, in his Carthage bishopric, seemed to him suggestive in pleasant reveries. More even than his works did the man attract him.

He had, in fact, lived in stormy times, agitated by frightful disorders, under Caracalla, under Macrinus, under the astonishing High Priest of Emesa, Elagabalus, and he tranquilly prepared his sermons, his dogmatic writings, his pleadings, his homilies, while the Roman Empire shook on its foundations, while the follies of Asia, while the ordures of paganism were full to the brim. With the utmost sang-froid, he recommended carnal abstinence, frugality in food, sobriety in dress, while, walking in silver powder and golden sand, a tiara on his head, his garb figured with precious stones, Elagabalus worked, amid his eunuchs, at womanish labor, calling himself the Empress and changing, every night, his Emperor, whom he preferably chose among barbers, scullions and circus drivers.

This antithesis delighted him. Then the Latin language, arrived at its supreme maturity under Petronius, commenced to decay; the Christian literature replaced it, bringing new words with new ideas, unemployed constructions, strange verbs, adjectives with subtle meanings, abstract words until then rare in the Roman language and whose usage Tertullian had been one of the first to adopt.

But there was no attraction in this dissolution, continued after Tertullian's death by his pupil, Saint Cyprian, by Arnobius and by Lactantius. There was something lacking; it made clumsy returns to Ciceronian magniloquence, but had not yet acquired that special flavor which in the fourth century, and particularly during the centuries following, the odor of Christianity would give the pagan tongue, decomposed like old venison, crumbling at the same time that the old world civilization collapsed, and the Empires, putrefied by the sanies of the centuries, succumbed to the thrusts of the barbarians.

Only one Christian poet, Commodianus, represented the third century in his library. The Carmen apologeticum, written in 259, is a collection of instructions, twisted into acrostics, in popular hexameters, with cæsuras introduced according to the heroic verse style, composed without regard to quantity or hiatus and often accompanied by such rhymes as the Church Latin would later supply in such abundance.

These sombre, tortuous, gamy verses, crammed with terms of ordinary speech, with words diverted from their primitive meaning, claimed and interested him even more than the soft and already green style of the historians, Ammianus Marcellinus and Aurelius Victorus, Symmachus the letter writer, and Macrobius the grammarian and compiler. Them he even preferred to the genuinely scanned lines, the spotted and superb language of Claudian, Rutilius and Ausonius.

They were then the masters of art. They filled the dying Empire with their cries; the Christian Ausonius with his Centon Nuptial, and his exuberant, embellished Mosella; Rutilius, with his hymns to the glory of Rome, his anathemas against the Jews and the monks, his journey from Italy into Gaul and the impressions recorded along the way, the intervals of landscape reflected in the water, the mirage of vapors and the movement of mists that enveloped the mountains.

Claudian, a sort of avatar of Lucan, dominates the fourth century with the terrible clarion of his verses: a poet forging a loud and sonorous hexameter, striking the epithet with a sharp blow amid sheaves of sparks, achieving a certain grandeur which fills his work with a powerful breath. In the Occidental Empire tottering more and more in the perpetual menace of the Barbarians now pressing in hordes at the Empire's yielding gates, he revives antiquity, sings of the abduction of Proserpine, lays on his vibrant colors and passes with all his torches alight, into the obscurity that was then engulfing his world.

Paganism again lives in his verse, sounding its last fanfare, lifting its last great poet above the Christianity which was soon entirely to submerge the language, and which would forever be sole master of art. The new Christian spirit arose with Paulinus, disciple of Ausonius; Juvencus, who paraphrases the gospels in verse; Victorinus, author of the Maccabees; Sanctus Burdigalensis who, in an eclogue imitated from Vergil, makes his shepherds Egon and Buculus lament the maladies of their flock; and all the saints: Hilaire of Poitiers, defender of the Nicean faith, the Athanasius of the Occident, as he has been called; Ambrosius, author of the indigestible homelies, the wearisome Christian Cicero; Damasus, maker of lapidary epigrams; Jerome, translator of the Vulgate, and his adversary Vigilantius, who attacks the cult of saints and the abuse of miracles and fastings, and already preaches, with arguments which future ages were to repeat, against the monastic vows and celibacy of the priests.

Finally, in the fifth century came Augustine, bishop of Hippo. Des Esseintes knew him only too well, for he was the Church's most reputed writer, founder of Christian orthodoxy, considered an oracle and sovereign master by Catholics. He no longer opened the pages of this holy man's works, although he had sung his disgust of the earth in the Confessions, and although his lamenting piety had essayed, in the City of God, to mitigate the frightful distress of the times by sedative promises of a rosier future. When Des Esseintes had studied theology, he was already sick and weary of the old monk's preachings and jeremiads, his theories on predestination and grace, his combats against the schisms.

He preferred to thumb the Psychomachia of Prudentius, that first type of the allegorical poem which was later, in the Middle Ages, to be used continually, and the works of Sidonius Apollinaris whose correspondence interlarded with flashes of wit, pungencies, archaisms and enigmas, allured him. He willingly re-read the panegyrics in which this bishop invokes pagan deities in substantiation of his vainglorious eulogies; and, in spite of everything, he confessed a weakness for the affectations of these verses, fabricated, as it were, by an ingenious mechanician who operates his machine, oils his wheels and invents intricate and useless parts.

After Sidonius, he sought Merobaudes, the panegyrist; Sedulius, author of the rhymed poems and abecedarian hymns, certain passages of which the Church has appropriated for its services; Marius Victorius, whose gloomy treatise on the Pervesity of the Times is illumed, here and there, with verses that gleam with phosphorescence; Paulinus of Pella, poet of the shivering Eucharisticon; and Orientius, bishop of Auch, who, in the distichs of his Monitories, inveighs against the licentiousness of women whose faces, he claims, corrupt the people.

The interest which Des Esseintes felt for the Latin language did not pause at this period which found it drooping, thoroughly putrid, losing its members and dropping its pus, and barely preserving through all the corruption of its body, those still firm elements which the Christians detached to marinate in the brine of their new language.

The second half of the fifth century had arrived, the horrible epoch when frightful motions convulsed the earth. The Barbarians sacked Gaul. Paralyzed Rome, pillaged by the Visigoths, felt its life grow feeble, perceived its extremities, the occident and the orient, writhe in blood and grow more exhausted from day to day.

In this general dissolution, in the successive assassination of the Caesars, in the turmoil of carnage from one end of Europe to another, there resounded a terrible shout of triumph, stifling all clamors, silencing all voices. On the banks of the Danube, thousands of men astride on small horses, clad in rat-skin coats, monstrous Tartars with enormous heads, flat noses, chins gullied with scars and gashes, and jaundiced faces bare of hair, rushed at full speed to envelop the territories of the Lower Empire like a whirlwind.

Everything disappeared in the dust of their gallopings, in the smoke of the conflagrations. Darkness fell, and the amazed people trembled, as they heard the fearful tornado which passed with thunder crashes. The hordes of Huns razed Europe, rushed toward Gaul, overran the plains of Chalons where Aetius pillaged it in an awful charge. The plains, gorged with blood, foamed like a purple sea. Two hundred thousand corpses barred the way, broke the movement of this avalanche which, swerving, fell with mighty thunderclaps, against Italy whose exterminated towns flamed like burning bricks.

The Occidental Empire crumbled beneath the shock; the moribund life which it was pursuing to imbecility and foulness, was extinguished. For another reason, the end of the universe seemed near; such cities as had been forgotten by Attila were decimated by famine and plague. The Latin language in its turn, seemed to sink under the world's ruins.

Years hastened on. The Barbarian idioms began to be modulated, to leave their vein-stones and form real languages. Latin, saved in the debacle by the cloisters, was confined in its usage to the convents and monasteries.

Here and there some poets gleamed, dully and coldly: the African Dracontius with his Hexameron, Claudius Memertius, with his liturgical poetry; Avitus of Vienne; then, the biographers like Ennodius, who narrates the prodigies of that perspicacious and venerated diplomat, Saint Epiphanius, the upright and vigilant pastor; or like Eugippus, who tells of the life of Saint Severin, that mysterious hermit and humble ascetic who appeared like an angel of grace to the distressed people, mad with suffering and fear; writers like Veranius of Gevaudan who prepared a little treatise on continence; like Aurelianus and Ferreolus who compiled the ecclesiastical canons; historians like Rotherius, famous for a lost history of the Huns.

Des Esseintes' library did not contain many works of the centuries immediately succeeding. Notwithstanding this deficiency, the sixth century was represented by Fortunatus, bishop of Poitiers, whose hymns and Vexila regis, carved out of the old carrion of the Latin language and spiced with the aromatics of the Church, haunted him on certain days; by Boethius, Gregory of Tours, and Jornandez. In the seventh and eighth centuries since, in addition to the low Latin of the Chroniclers, the Fredegaires and Paul Diacres, and the poems contained in the Bangor antiphonary which he sometimes read for the alphabetical and mono-rhymed hymn sung in honor of Saint Comgill, the literature limited itself almost exclusively to biographies of saints, to the legend of Saint Columban, written by the monk, Jonas, and to that of the blessed Cuthbert, written by the Venerable Bede from the notes of an anonymous monk of Lindisfarn, he contented himself with glancing over, in his moments of tedium, the works of these hagiographers and in again reading several extracts from the lives of Saint Rusticula and Saint Radegonda, related, the one by Defensorius, the other by the modest and ingenious Baudonivia, a nun of Poitiers.

But the singular works of Latin and Anglo-Saxon literature allured him still further. They included the whole series of riddles by Adhelme, Tatwine and Eusebius, who were descendants of Symphosius, and especially the enigmas composed by Saint Boniface, in acrostic strophes whose solution could be found in the initial letters of the verses.

His interest diminished with the end of those two centuries. Hardly pleased with the cumbersome mass of Carlovingian Latinists, the Alcuins and the Eginhards, he contented himself, as a specimen of the language of the ninth century, with the chronicles of Saint Gall, Freculfe and Reginon; with the poem of the siege of Paris written by Abbo le Courbe; with the didactic Hortulus, of the Benedictine Walafrid Strabo, whose chapter consecrated to the glory of the gourd as a symbol of fruitfulness, enlivened him; with the poem in which Ermold the Dark, celebrating the exploits of Louis the Debonair, a poem written in regular hexameters, in an austere, almost forbidding style and in a Latin of iron dipped in monastic waters with straws of sentiment, here and there, in the unpliant metal; with the De viribus herbarum, the poem of Macer Floridus, who particularly delighted him because of his poetic recipes and the very strange virtues which he ascribes to certain plants and flowers; to the aristolochia, for example, which, mixed with the flesh of a cow and placed on the lower part of a pregnant woman's abdomen, insures the birth of a male child; or to the borage which, when brewed into an infusion in a dining room, diverts guests; or to the peony whose powdered roots cure epilepsy; or to the fennel which, if placed on a woman's breasts, clears her water and stimulates the indolence of her periods.

Apart from several special, unclassified volumes, modern or dateless, certain works on the Cabbala, medicine and botany, certain odd tomes containing undiscoverable Christian poetry, and the anthology of the minor Latin poets of Wernsdorf; apart from Meursius, the manual of classical erotology of Forberg, and the diaconals used by confessors, which he dusted at rare intervals, his Latin library ended at the beginning of the tenth century.

And, in fact, the curiosity, the complicated naïveté of the Christian language had also foundered. The balderdash of philosophers and scholars, the logomachy of the Middle Ages, thenceforth held absolute sway. The sooty mass of chronicles and historical books and cartularies accumulated, and the stammering grace, the often exquisite awkwardness of the monks, placing the poetic remains of antiquity in a ragout, were dead. The fabrications of verbs and purified essences, of substantives breathing of incense, of bizarre adjectives, coarsely carved from gold, with the barbarous and charming taste of Gothic jewels, were destroyed. The old editions, beloved by Des Esseintes, here ended; and with a formidable leap of centuries, the books on his shelves went straight to the French language of the present century.

Chapter 5

The afternoon was drawing to its close when a carriage halted in front of the Fontenay house. Since Des Esseintes received no visitors, and since the postman never even ventured into these uninhabited parts, having no occasion to deliver any papers, magazines or letters, the servants hesitated before opening the door. Then, as the bell was rung furiously again, they peered through the peep-hole cut into the wall, and perceived a man, concealed, from neck to waist, behind an immense gold buckler.

They informed their master, who was breakfasting.

"Ask him in," he said, for he recalled having given his address to a lapidary for the delivery of a purchase.

The man bowed and deposited the buckler on the pinewood floor of the dining room. It oscillated and wavered, revealing the serpentine head of a tortoise which, suddenly terrified, retreated into its shell.

This tortoise was a fancy which had seized Des Esseintes some time before his departure from Paris. Examining an Oriental rug, one day, in reflected light, and following the silver gleams which fell on its web of plum violet and alladin yellow, it suddenly occurred to him how much it would be improved if he could place on it some object whose deep color might enhance the vividness of its tints.

Possessed by this idea, he had been strolling aimlessly along the streets, when suddenly he found himself gazing at the very object of his wishes. There, in a shop window on the Palais Royal, lay a huge tortoise in a large basin. He had purchased it. Then he had sat a long time, with eyes half-shut, studying the effect.

Decidedly, the Ethiopic black, the harsh Sienna tone of this shell dulled the rug's reflections without adding to it. The dominant silver gleams in it barely sparkled, crawling with lack-lustre tones of dead zinc against the edges of the hard, tarnished shell.

He bit his nails while he studied a method of removing these discords and reconciling the determined opposition of the tones. He finally discovered that his first inspiration, which was to animate the fire of the weave by setting it off against some dark object, was erroneous. In fact, this rug was too new, too petulant and gaudy. The colors were not sufficiently subdued. He must reverse the process, dull the tones, and extinguish them by the contrast of a striking object, which would eclipse all else and cast a golden light on the pale silver. Thus stated, the problem was easier to solve. He therefore decided to glaze the shell of the tortoise with gold.

The tortoise, just returned by the lapidary, shone brilliantly, softening the tones of the rug and casting on it a gorgeous reflection which resembled the irradiations from the scales of a barbaric Visigoth shield.

At first Des Esseintes was enchanted with this effect. Then he reflected that this gigantic jewel was only in outline, that it would not really be complete until it had been incrusted with rare stones.

From a Japanese collection he chose a design representing a cluster of flowers emanating spindle-like, from a slender stalk. Taking it to a jeweler, he sketched a border to enclose this bouquet in an oval frame, and informed the amazed lapidary that every petal and every leaf was to be designed with jewels and mounted on the scales of the tortoise.

The choice of stones made him pause. The diamond has become notoriously common since every tradesman has taken to wearing it on his little finger. The oriental emeralds and rubies are less vulgarized and cast brilliant, rutilant flames, but they remind one of the green and red antennæ of certain omnibuses which carry signal lights of these colors. As for topazes, whether sparkling or dim, they are cheap stones, precious only to women of the middle class who like to have jewel cases on their dressing-tables. And then, although the Church has preserved for the amethyst a sacerdotal character which is at once unctuous and solemn, this stone, too, is abused on the blood-red ears and veined hands of butchers' wives who love to adorn themselves inexpensively with real and heavy jewels. Only the sapphire, among all these stones, has kept its fires undefiled by any taint of commercialism. Its sparks, crackling in its limpid, cold depths have in some way protected its shy and proud nobility from pollution. Unfortunately, its fresh fire does not sparkle in artificial light: the blue retreats and seems to fall asleep, only awakening to shine at daybreak.

None of these satisfied Des Esseintes at all. They were too civilized and familiar. He let trickle through his fingers still more astonishing and bizarre stones, and finally selected a number of real and artificial ones which, used together, should produce a fascinating and disconcerting harmony.

This is how he composed his bouquet of flowers: the leaves were set with jewels of a pronounced, distinct green; the chrysoberyls of asparagus green; the chrysolites of leek green; the olivines of olive green. They hung from branches of almandine and ouwarovite of a violet red, darting spangles of a hard brilliance like tartar micas gleaming through forest depths.

For the flowers, separated from the stalk and removed from the bottom of the sheaf, he used blue cinder. But he formally waived that oriental turquoise used for brooches and rings which, like the banal pearl and the odious coral, serves to delight people of no importance. He chose occidental turquoises exclusively, stones which, properly speaking, are only a fossil ivory impregnated with coppery substances whose sea blue is choked, opaque, sulphurous, as though yellowed by bile.

This done, he could now set the petals of his flowers with transparent stones which had morbid and vitreous sparks, feverish and sharp lights.

He composed them entirely with Ceylon snap-dragons, cymophanes and blue chalcedony.

These three stones darted mysterious and perverse scintillations, painfully torn from the frozen depths of their troubled waters.

The snap-dragon of a greenish grey, streaked with concentric veins which seem to stir and change constantly, according to the dispositions of light.

The cymophane, whose azure waves float over the milky tint swimming in its depths.

The blue chalcedony which kindles with bluish phosphorescent fires against a dead brown, chocolate background.

The lapidary made a note of the places where the stones were to be inlaid. "And the border of the shell?" he asked Des Esseintes.

At first he had thought of some opals and hydrophanes; but these stones, interesting for their hesitating colors, for the evasions of their flames, are too refractory and faithless; the opal has a quite rheumatic sensitiveness; the play of its rays alters according to the humidity, the warmth or cold; as for the hydrophane, it only burns in water and only consents to kindle its embers when moistened.

He finally decided on minerals whose reflections vary; for the Compostelle hyacinth, mahogany red; the beryl, glaucous green; the balas ruby, vinegar rose; the Sudermanian ruby, pale slate. Their feeble sparklings sufficed to light the darkness of the shell and preserved the values of the flowering stones which they encircled with a slender garland of vague fires.

Des Esseintes now watched the tortoise squatting in a corner of the dining room, shining in the shadow.

He was perfectly happy. His eyes gleamed with pleasure at the resplendencies of the flaming corrollæ against the gold background. Then, he grew hungry—a thing that rarely if ever happened to him—and dipped his toast, spread with a special butter, in a cup of tea, a flawless blend of Siafayoune, Moyoutann and Khansky—yellow teas which had come from China to Russia by special caravans.

This liquid perfume he drank in those Chinese porcelains called egg-shell, so light and diaphanous they are. And, as an accompaniment to these adorable cups, he used a service of solid silver, slightly gilded; the silver showed faintly under the fatigued layer of gold, which gave it an aged, quite exhausted and moribund tint.

After he had finished his tea, he returned to his study and had the servant carry in the tortoise which stubbornly refused to budge.

The snow was falling. By the lamp light, he saw the icy patterns on the bluish windows, and the hoar-frost, like melted sugar, scintillating in the stumps of bottles spotted with gold.

A deep silence enveloped the cottage drooping in shadow.

Des Esseintes fell into revery. The fireplace piled with logs gave forth a smell of burning wood. He opened the window slightly.

Like a high tapestry of black ermine, the sky rose before him, black flecked with white.

An icy wind swept past, accelerated the crazy flight of the snow, and reversed the color order.

The heraldic tapestry of heaven returned, became a true ermine, a white flecked with black, in its turn, by the specks of darkness dispersed among the flakes.

He closed the window. This abrupt transition from torrid warmth to cold winter affected him. He crouched near the fire and it occurred to him that he needed a cordial to revive his flagging spirits.

He went to the dining room where, built in one of the panels, was a closet containing a number of tiny casks, ranged side by side, and resting on small stands of sandal wood.

This collection of barrels he called his mouth organ.

A stem could connect all the spigots and control them by a single movement, so that once attached, he had only to press a button concealed in the woodwork to turn on all the taps at the same time and fill the mugs placed underneath.

The organ was now open. The stops labelled flute, horn, celestial voice, were pulled out, ready to be placed. Des Esseintes sipped here and there, enjoying the inner symphonies, succeeded in procuring sensations in his throat analogous to those which music gives to the ear.

Moreover, each liquor corresponded, according to his thinking, to the sound of some instrument. Dry curacoa, for example, to the clarinet whose tone is sourish and velvety; kümmel to the oboe whose sonorous notes snuffle; mint and anisette to the flute, at once sugary and peppery, puling and sweet; while, to complete the orchestra, kirschwasser has the furious ring of the trumpet; gin and whiskey burn the palate with their strident crashings of trombones and cornets; brandy storms with the deafening hubbub of tubas; while the thunder-claps of the cymbals and the furiously beaten drum roll in the mouth by means of the rakis de Chio.

He also thought that the comparison could be continued, that quartets of string instruments could play under the palate, with the violin simulated by old brandy, fumous and fine, piercing and frail; the tenor violin by rum, louder and more sonorous; the cello by the lacerating and lingering ratafia, melancholy and caressing; with the double-bass, full-bodied, solid and dark as the old bitters. If one wished to form a quintet, one could even add a fifth instrument with the vibrant taste, the silvery detached and shrill note of dry cumin imitating the harp.

The comparison was further prolonged. Tone relationships existed in the music of liquors; to cite but one note, benedictine represents, so to speak, the minor key of that major key of alcohols which are designated in commercial scores, under the name of green Chartreuse.

These principles once admitted, he succeeded, after numerous experiments, in enjoying silent melodies on his tongue, mute funeral marches, in hearing, in his mouth, solos of mint, duos of ratafia and rum.

He was even able to transfer to his palate real pieces of music, following the composer step by step, rendering his thought, his effects, his nuances, by combinations or contrasts of liquors, by approximative and skilled mixtures.

At other times, he himself composed melodies, executed pastorals with mild black-currant which evoked, in his throat, the trillings of nightingales; with the tender chouva cocoa which sang saccharine songs like "The romance of Estelle" and the "Ah! Shall I tell you, mama," of past days.

But on this evening Des Esseintes was not inclined to listen to this music. He confined himself to sounding one note on the keyboard of his organ, by swallowing a little glass of genuine Irish whiskey.

He sank into his easy chair and slowly inhaled this fermented juice of oats and barley: a pronounced taste of creosote was in his mouth.

Gradually, as he drank, his thought followed the now revived sensitiveness of his palate, fitted its progress to the flavor of the whiskey, re-awakened, by a fatal exactitude of odors, memories effaced for years.

This carbolic tartness forcibly recalled to him the same taste he had had on his tongue in the days when dentists worked on his gums.

Once abandoned on this track, his revery, at first dispersed among all the dentists he had known, concentrated and converged on one of them who was more firmly engraved in his memory.

It had happened three years ago. Seized, in the middle of the night, with an abominable toothache, he put his hand to his cheek, stumbled against the furniture, pacing up and down the room like a demented person.

It was a molar which had already been filled; no remedy was possible. Only a dentist could alleviate the pain. He feverishly waited for the day, resolved to bear the most atrocious operation provided it would only ease his sufferings.

Holding a hand to his jaw, he asked himself what should be done. The dentists who treated him were rich merchants whom one could not see at any time; one had to make an appointment. He told himself that this would never do, that he could not endure it. He decided to patronize the first one he could find, to hasten to a popular tooth-extractor, one of those iron-fisted men who, if they are ignorant of the useless art of dressing decaying teeth and of filling holes, know how to pull the stubbornest stump with an unequalled rapidity. There, the office is opened early in the morning and one is not required to wait. Seven o'clock struck at last. He hurried out, and recollecting the name of a mechanic who called himself a dentist and dwelt in the corner of a quay, he rushed through the streets, holding his cheek with his hands repressing the tears.

Arrived in front of the house, recognizable by an immense wooden signboard where the name of "Gatonax" sprawled in enormous pumpkin-colored letters, and by two little glass cases where false teeth were carefully set in rose-colored wax, he gasped for breath. He perspired profusely. A horrible fear shook him, a trembling crept under his skin; suddenly a calm ensued, the suffering ceased, the tooth stopped paining.

He remained, stupefied, on the sidewalk; finally, he stiffened against the anguish, mounted the dim stairway, running up four steps at a time to the fourth story. He found himself in front of a door where an enamel plate repeated, inscribed in sky-blue lettering, the name on the signboard. He rang the bell and then, terrified by the great red spittles which he noticed on the steps, he faced about, resolved to endure his toothache all his life. At that moment an excruciating cry pierced the partitions, filled the cage of the doorway and glued him to the spot with horror, at the same time that a door was opened and an old woman invited him to enter.

His feeling of shame quickly changed to fear. He was ushered into a dining room. Another door creaked and in entered a terrible grenadier dressed in a frock-coat and black trousers. Des Esseintes followed him to another room.

From this instant, his sensations were confused. He vaguely remembered having sunk into a chair opposite a window, having murmured, as he put a finger to his tooth: "It has already been filled and I am afraid nothing more can be done with it."

The man immediately suppressed these explanations by introducing an enormous index finger into his mouth. Muttering beneath his waxed fang-like moustaches, he took an instrument from the table.

Then the play began. Clinging to the arms of his seat, Des Esseintes felt a cold sensation in his cheek, and began to suffer unheard agonies. Then he beheld stars. He stamped his feet frantically and bleated like a sheep about to be slaughtered.

A snapping sound was heard, the molar had broken while being extracted. It seemed that his head was being shattered, that his skull was being smashed; he lost his senses, howled as loudly as he could, furiously defending himself from the man who rushed at him anew as if he wished to implant his whole arm in the depths of his bowels, brusquely recoiled a step and, lifting the tooth attached to the jaw, brutally let him fall back into the chair. Breathing heavily, his form filling the window, he brandished at one end of his forceps, a blue tooth with blood at one end.

Faint and prostrate, Des Esseintes spat blood into a basin, refused with a gesture, the tooth which the old woman was about to wrap in a piece of paper and fled, after paying two francs. Expectorating blood, in his turn, down the steps, he at length found himself in the street, joyous, feeling ten years younger, interested in every little occurrence.

"Phew!" he exclaimed, saddened by the assault of these memories. He rose to dissipate the horrible spell of this vision and, returning to reality, began to be concerned with the tortoise.

It did not budge at all and he tapped it. The animal was dead. Doubtless accustomed to a sedentary existence, to a humble life spent underneath its poor shell, it had been unable to support the dazzling luxury imposed on it, the rutilant cope with which it had been covered, the jewels with which its back had been paved, like a pyx.

Chapter 6

With the sharpening of his desire to withdraw from a hated age, he felt a despotic urge to shun pictures representing humanity striving in little holes or running to and fro in quest of money.

With his growing indifference to contemporary life he had resolved not to introduce into his cell any of the ghosts of distastes or regrets, but had desired to procure subtle and exquisite paintings, steeped in ancient dreams or antique corruptions, far removed from the manner of our present day.

For the delight of his spirit and the joy of his eyes, he had desired a few suggestive creations that cast him into an unknown world, revealing to him the contours of new conjectures, agitating the nervous system by the violent deliriums, complicated nightmares, nonchalant or atrocious chimeræ they induced.

Among these were some executed by an artist whose genius allured and entranced him: Gustave Moreau.

Des Esseintes had acquired his two masterpieces and, at night, used to sink into revery before one of them—a representation of Salomé, conceived in this fashion:

A throne, resembling the high altar of a cathedral, reared itself beneath innumerable vaults leaping from heavy Romanesque pillars, studded with polychromatic bricks, set with mosaics, incrusted with lapis lazuli and sardonyx, in a palace that, like a basilica, was at once Mohammedan and Byzantine in design.

In the center of the tabernacle, surmounting an altar approached by semi-circular steps, sat Herod the Tetrarch, a tiara upon his head, his legs pressed closely together, his hands resting upon his knees.

His face was the color of yellow parchment; it was furrowed with wrinkles, ravaged with age. His long beard floated like a white cloud upon the star-like clusters of jewels constellating the orphrey robe fitting tightly over his breast.

Around this form, frozen into the immobile, sacerdotal, hieratic pose of a Hindoo god, burned perfumes wafting aloft clouds of incense which were perforated, like phosphorescent eyes of beasts, by the fiery rays of the stones set in the throne. Then the vapor rolled up, diffusing itself beneath arcades where the blue smoke mingled with the gold powder of the long sunbeams falling from the domes.

In the perverse odor of the perfumes, in the overheated atmosphere of the temple, Salomé, her left arm outstretched in a gesture of command, her right arm drawn back and holding a large lotus on a level with her face, slowly advances on her toes, to the rhythm of a stringed instrument played by a woman seated on the ground.

Her face is meditative, solemn, almost august, as she commences the lascivious dance that will awaken the slumbering senses of old Herod. Diamonds scintillate against her glistening skin. Her bracelets, her girdles, her rings flash. On her triumphal robe, seamed with pearls, flowered with silver and laminated with gold, the breastplate of jewels, each link of which is a precious stone, flashes serpents of fire against the pallid flesh, delicate as a tea-rose: its jewels like splendid insects with dazzling elytra, veined with carmine, dotted with yellow gold, diapered with blue steel, speckled with peacock green.

With a tense concentration, with the fixed gaze of a somnambulist, she beholds neither the trembling Tetrarch, nor her mother, the fierce Herodias who watches her, nor the hermaphrodite, nor the eunuch who sits, sword in hand, at the foot of the throne—a terrible figure, veiled to his eyes, whose breasts droop like gourds under his orange-checkered tunic.

This conception of Salomé, so haunting to artists and poets, had obsessed Des Esseintes for years. How often had he read in the old Bible of Pierre Variquet, translated by the theological doctors of the University of Louvain, the Gospel of Saint Matthew who, in brief and ingenuous phrases, recounts the beheading of the Baptist! How often had he fallen into revery, as he read these lines:

But when Herod's birthday was kept, the daughter of Herodias danced before them, and pleased Herod.

Whereupon he promised with an oath to give her whatsoever she would ask.

And she, being before instructed of her mother, said: Give me here John Baptist's head in a charger.

And the king was sorry: nevertheless, for the oath's sake, and them which sat with him at meat, he commanded it to be given her.

And he sent, and beheaded John in the prison.

And his head was brought in a charger, and given to the damsel: and she brought it to her mother.

But neither Saint Matthew, nor Saint Mark, nor Saint Luke, nor the other Evangelists had emphasized the maddening charms and depravities of the dancer. She remained vague and hidden, mysterious and swooning in the far-off mist of the centuries, not to be grasped by vulgar and materialistic minds, accessible only to disordered and volcanic intellects made visionaries by their neuroticism; rebellious to painters of the flesh, to Rubens who disguised her as a butcher's wife of Flanders; a mystery to all the writers who had never succeeded in portraying the disquieting exaltation of this dancer, the refined grandeur of this murderess.

In Gustave Moreau's work, conceived independently of the Testament themes, Des Esseintes as last saw realized the superhuman and exotic Salomé of his dreams. She was no longer the mere performer who wrests a cry of desire and of passion from an old man by a perverted twisting of her loins; who destroys the energy and breaks the will of a king by trembling breasts and quivering belly. She became, in a sense, the symbolic deity of indestructible lust, the goddess of immortal Hysteria, of accursed Beauty, distinguished from all others by the catalepsy which stiffens her flesh and hardens her muscles; the monstrous Beast, indifferent, irresponsible, insensible, baneful, like the Helen of antiquity, fatal to all who approach her, all who behold her, all whom she touches.

Thus understood, she was associated with the theogonies of the Far East. She no longer sprang from biblical traditions, could no longer even be assimilated with the living image of Babylon, the royal Prostitute of the Apocalypse, garbed like her in jewels and purple, and painted like her; for she was not hurled by a fatidical power, by a supreme force, into the alluring vileness of debauchery.

The painter, moreover, seems to have wished to affirm his desire of remaining outside the centuries, scorning to designate the origin, nation and epoch, by placing his Salomé in this extraordinary palace with its confused and imposing style, in clothing her with sumptuous and chimerical robes, in crowning her with a fantastic mitre shaped like a Phœnician tower, such as Salammbô bore, and placing in her hand the sceptre of Isis, the tall lotus, sacred flower of Egypt and India.

Des Esseintes sought the sense of this emblem. Had it that phallic significance which the primitive cults of India gave it? Did it enunciate an oblation of virginity to the senile Herod, an exchange of blood, an impure and voluntary wound, offered under the express stipulation of a monstrous sin? Or did it represent the allegory of fecundity, the Hindoo myth of life, an existence held between the hands of woman, distorted and trampled by the palpitant hands of man whom a fit of madness seizes, seduced by a convulsion of the flesh?

Perhaps, too, in arming his enigmatic goddess with the venerated lotus, the painter had dreamed of the dancer, the mortal woman with the polluted Vase, from whom spring all sins and crimes. Perhaps he had recalled the rites of ancient Egypt, the sepulchral ceremonies of the embalming when, after stretching the corpse on a bench of jasper, extracting the brain with curved needles through the chambers of the nose, the chemists and the priests, before gilding the nails and teeth and coating the body with bitumens and essences, inserted the chaste petals of the divine flower in the sexual parts, to purify them.

However this may be, an irresistible fascination emanated from this painting; but the water-color entitled The Apparition was perhaps even more disturbing.

There, the palace of Herod arose like an Alhambra on slender, iridescent columns with moorish tile, joined with silver beton and gold cement. Arabesques proceeded from lozenges of lapis lazuli, wove their patterns on the cupolas where, on nacreous marquetry, crept rainbow gleams and prismatic flames.

The murder was accomplished. The executioner stood impassive, his hands on the hilt of his long, blood-stained sword.

The severed head of the saint stared lividly on the charger resting on the slabs; the mouth was discolored and open, the neck crimson, and tears fell from the eyes. The face was encircled by an aureole worked in mosaic, which shot rays of light under the porticos and illuminated the horrible ascension of the head, brightening the glassy orbs of the contracted eyes which were fixed with a ghastly stare upon the dancer.

With a gesture of terror, Salomé thrusts from her the horrible vision which transfixes her, motionless, to the ground. Her eyes dilate, her hands clasp her neck in a convulsive clutch.

She is almost nude. In the ardor of the dance, her veils had become loosened. She is garbed only in gold-wrought stuffs and limpid stones; a neck-piece clasps her as a corselet does the body and, like a superb buckle, a marvelous jewel sparkles on the hollow between her breasts. A girdle encircles her hips, concealing the upper part of her thighs, against which beats a gigantic pendant streaming with carbuncles and emeralds.

All the facets of the jewels kindle under the ardent shafts of light escaping from the head of the Baptist. The stones grow warm, outlining the woman's body with incandescent rays, striking her neck, feet and arms with tongues of fire,—vermilions like coals, violets like jets of gas, blues like flames of alcohol, and whites like star light.

The horrible head blazes, bleeding constantly, clots of sombre purple on the ends of the beard and hair. Visible for Salomé alone, it does not, with its fixed gaze, attract Herodias, musing on her finally consummated revenge, nor the Tetrarch who, bent slightly forward, his hands on his knees, still pants, maddened by the nudity of the woman saturated with animal odors, steeped in balms, exuding incense and myrrh.

Like the old king, Des Esseintes remained dumbfounded, overwhelmed and seized with giddiness, in the presence of this dancer who was less majestic, less haughty but more disquieting than the Salomé of the oil painting.

In this insensate and pitiless image, in this innocent and dangerous idol, the eroticism and terror of mankind were depicted. The tall lotus had disappeared, the goddess had vanished; a frightful nightmare now stifled the woman, dizzied by the whirlwind of the dance, hypnotized and petrified by terror.

It was here that she was indeed Woman, for here she gave rein to her ardent and cruel temperament. She was living, more refined and savage, more execrable and exquisite. She more energetically awakened the dulled senses of man, more surely bewitched and subdued his power of will, with the charm of a tall venereal flower, cultivated in sacrilegious beds, in impious hothouses.

Des Esseintes thought that never before had a water color attained such magnificent coloring; never before had the poverty of colors been able to force jeweled corruscations from paper, gleams like stained glass windows touched by rays of sunlight, splendors of tissue and flesh so fabulous and dazzling. Lost in contemplation, he sought to discover the origins of this great artist and mystic pagan, this visionary who succeeded in removing himself from the world sufficiently to behold, here in Paris, the splendor of these cruel visions and the enchanting sublimation of past ages.

Des Esseintes could not trace the genesis of this artist. Here and there were vague suggestions of Mantegna and of Jacopo de Barbari; here and there were confused hints of Vinci and of the feverish colors of Delacroix. But the influences of such masters remained negligible. The fact was that Gustave Moreau derived from no one else. He remained unique in contemporary art, without ancestors and without possible descendants. He went to ethnographic sources, to the origins of myths, and he compared and elucidated their intricate enigmas. He reunited the legends of the Far East into a whole, the myths which had been altered by the superstitions of other peoples; thus justifying his architectonic fusions, his luxurious and outlandish fabrics, his hieratic and sinister allegories sharpened by the restless perceptions of a pruriently modern neurosis. And he remained saddened, haunted by the symbols of perversities and superhuman loves, of divine stuprations brought to end without abandonment and without hope.

His depressing and erudite productions possessed a strange enchantment, an incantation that stirred one to the depths, just as do certain poems of Baudelaire, caused one to pause disconcerted, amazed, brooding on the spell of an art which leaped beyond the confines of painting, borrowing its most subtle effects from the art of writing, its most marvelous stokes from the art of Limosin, its most exquisite refinements from the art of the lapidary and the engraver. These two pictures of Salomé, for which Des Esseintes' admiration was boundless, he had hung on the walls of his study on special panels between the bookshelves, so that they might live under his eyes.

But these were not the only pictures he had acquired to divert his solitude.

Although he had surrendered to his servants the second story of his house, which he himself never used at all, the ground floor had required a number of pictures to fit the walls.

It was thus arranged:

A dressing room, communicating with the bedroom, occupied one of the corners of the house. One passed from the bedroom to the library, and from the library into the dining room, which formed the other corner.

These rooms, whose windows looked out on the Aunay Valley, composed one of the sides of the dwelling.

The other side of the house had four rooms arranged in the same order. Thus, the kitchen formed an angle, and corresponded with the dining room; a long corridor, which served as the entrance, with the library; a small dressing room, with the bedroom; and the toilet, forming a second angle, with the dressing room.

These rooms received the light from the side opposite the Aunay Valley and faced the Towers of Croy and Chatillon.

As for the staircase, it was built outside, against one of the sides of the house, and the footsteps of his servants in ascending or descending thus reached Des Esseintes less distinctly.

The dressing room was tapestried in deep red. On the walls, in ebony frames, hung the prints of Jan Luyken, an old Dutch engraver almost unknown in France.

He possessed of the work of this artist, who was fantastic and melancholy, vehement and wild, the series of his Religious Persecutions, horrible prints depicting all the agonies invented by the madness of religions: prints pregnant with human sufferings, showing bodies roasting on fires, skulls slit open with swords, trepaned with nails and gashed with saws, intestines separated from the abdomen and twisted on spools, finger nails slowly extracted with pincers, eyes gouged, limbs dislocated and deliberately broken, and bones bared of flesh and agonizingly scraped by sheets of metal.

These works filled with abominable imaginings, offensive with their odors of burning, oozing with blood and clamorous with cries of horror and maledictions, gave Des Esseintes, who was held fascinated in this red room, the creeping sensations of goose-flesh.

But in addition to the tremblings they occasioned, beyond the terrible skill of this man, the extraordinary life which animates his characters, one discovered, among his astonishing, swarming throngs—among his mobs of people delineated with a dexterity which recalled Callot, but which had a strength never possessed by that amusing dauber—curious reconstructions of bygone ages. The architecture, costumes and customs during the time of the Maccabeans, of Rome under the Christian persecutions, of Spain under the Inquisition, of France during the Middle Ages, at the time of Saint Bartholomew and the Dragonnades, were studied with a meticulous care and noted with scientific accuracy.

These prints were veritable treasures of learning. One could gaze at them for hours without experiencing any sense of weariness. Profoundly suggestive in reflections, they assisted Des Esseintes in passing many a day when his books failed to charm him.

Luyken's life, too, fascinated him, by explaining the hallucination of his work. A fervent Calvinist, a stubborn sectarian, unbalanced by prayers and hymns, he wrote religious poetry which he illustrated, paraphrased the psalms in verse, lost himself in the reading of the Bible from which he emerged haggard and frenzied, his brain haunted by monstrous subjects, his mouth twisted by the maledictions of the Reformation and by its songs of terror and hate.

And he scorned the world, surrendering his wealth to the poor and subsisting on a slice of bread. He ended his life in travelling, with an equally fanatical servant, going where chance led his boat, preaching the Gospel far and wide, endeavoring to forego nourishment, and eventually becoming almost demented and violent.

Other bizarre sketches were hung in the larger, adjoining room, as well as in the corridor, both of which had woodwork of red cedar.

There was Bresdin's Comedy of Death in which, in the fantastic landscape bristling with trees, brushwood and tufts of grass resembling phantom, demon forms, teeming with rat-headed, pod-tailed birds, on earth covered with ribs, skulls and bones, gnarled and cracked willows rear their trunks, surmounted by agitated skeletons whose arms beat the air while they intone a song of victory. A Christ speeds across a clouded sky; a hermit in the depths of a cave meditates, holding his head in his hands; one wretch dies, exhausted by long privation and enfeebled by hunger, lying on his back, his legs outstretched in front of a pond.

The Good Samaritan, by the same artist, is a large engraving on stone: an incongruous medley of palms, sorbs and oaks grown together, heedless of seasons and climates, peopled with monkeys and owls, covered with old stumps as misshapen as the roots of the mandrake; then a magical forest, cut in the center near a glade through which a stream can be seen far away, behind a camel and the Samaritan group; then an elfin town appearing on the horizon of an exotic sky dotted with birds and covered with masses of fleecy clouds.

It could be called the design of an uncertain, primitive Durer with an opium-steeped brain. But although he liked the finesse of the detail and the imposing appearance of this print, Des Esseintes had a special weakness for the other frames adorning the room.

They were signed: Odilon Redon.

They enclosed inconceivable apparitions in their rough, gold-striped pear-tree wood. A head of a Merovingian style, resting against a bowl, a bearded man, at once resembling a Buddhist priest and an orator at a public reunion, touching the ball of a gigantic cannon with his fingers; a frightful spider revealing a human face in its body. The charcoal drawings went even farther into dream terrors. Here, an enormous die in which a sad eye winked; there, dry and arid landscapes, dusty plains, shifting ground, volcanic upheavals catching rebellious clouds, stagnant and livid skies. Sometimes the subjects even seemed to have borrowed from the cacodemons of science, reverting to prehistoric times. A monstrous plant on the rocks, queer blocks everywhere, glacial mud, figures whose simian shapes, heavy jaws, beetling eyebrows, retreating foreheads and flat skulls, recalled the ancestral heads of the first quaternary periods, when inarticulate man still devoured fruits and seeds, and was still contemporaneous with the mammoth, the rhinoceros and the big bear. These designs were beyond anything imaginable; they leaped, for the most part, beyond the limits of painting and introduced a fantasy that was unique, the fantasy of a diseased and delirious mind.

And, indeed, certain of these faces, with their monstrous, insane eyes, certain of these swollen, deformed bodies resembling carafes, induced in Des Esseintes recollections of typhoid, memories of feverish nights and of the shocking visions of his infancy which persisted and would not be suppressed.

Seized with an indefinable uneasiness in the presence of these sketches, the same sensation caused by certain Proverbs of Goya which they recalled, or by the reading of Edgar Allen Poe's tales, whose mirages of hallucination and effects of fear Odilon Redon seemed to have transposed to a different art, he rubbed his eyes and turned to contemplate a radiant figure which, amid these tormenting sketches, arose serene and calm—a figure of Melancholy seated near the disk of a sun, on the rocks, in a dejected and gloomy posture.

The shadows were dispersed as though by an enchantment. A charming sadness, a languid and desolate feeling flowed through him. He meditated long before this work which, with its dashes of paint flecking the thick crayon, spread a brilliance of sea-green and of pale gold among the protracted darkness of the charcoal prints.

In addition to this series of the works of Redon which adorned nearly every panel of the passage, he had hung a disturbing sketch by El Greco in his bedroom. It was a Christ done in strange tints, in a strained design, possessing a wild color and a disordered energy: a picture executed in the painter's second manner when he had been tormented by the necessity of avoiding imitation of Titian.

This sinister painting, with its wax and sickly green tones, bore an affinity to certain ideas Des Esseintes had with regard to furnishing a room.

According to him, there were but two ways of fitting a bedroom. One could either make it a sense-stimulating alcove, a place for nocturnal delights, or a cell for solitude and repose, a retreat for thought, a sort of oratory.

For the first instance, the Louis XV style was inevitable for the fastidious, for the cerebrally morbid. Only the eighteenth century had succeeded in enveloping woman with a vicious atmosphere, imitating her contours in the undulations and twistings of wood and copper, accentuating the sugary languor of the blond with its clear and lively décors, attenuating the pungency of the brunette with its tapestries of aqueous, sweet, almost insipid tones.

He had once had such a room in Paris, with a lofty, white, lacquered bed which is one stimulant the more, a source of depravity to old roues, leering at the false chastity and hypocritical modesty of Greuze's tender virgins, at the deceptive candor of a bed evocative of babes and chaste maidens.

For the second instance,—and now that he wished to put behind him the irritating memories of his past life, this was the only possible expedient—he was compelled to design a room that would be like a monastic cell. But difficulties faced him here, for he refused to accept in its entirety the austere ugliness of those asylums of penitence and prayer.

By dint of studying the problem in all its phases, he concluded that the end to be attained could thus be stated: to devise a sombre effect by means of cheerful objects, or rather to give a tone of elegance and distinction to the room thus treated, meanwhile preserving its character of ugliness; to reverse the practice of the theatre, whose vile tinsel imitates sumptuous and costly textures; to obtain the contrary effect by use of splendid fabrics; in a word, to have the cell of a Carthusian monk which should possess the appearance of reality without in fact being so.

Thus he proceeded. To imitate the stone-color of ochre and clerical yellow, he had his walls covered with saffron silk; to stimulate the chocolate hue of the dadoes common to this type of room, he used pieces of violet wood deepened with amarinth. The effect was bewitching, while recalling to Des Esseintes the repellant rigidity of the model he had followed and yet transformed. The ceiling, in turn, was hung with white, unbleached cloth, in imitation of plaster, but without its discordant brightness. As for the cold pavement of the cell, he was able to copy it, by means of a bit of rug designed in red squares, with whitish spots in the weave to imitate the wear of sandals and the friction of boots.

Into this chamber he introduced a small iron bed, the kind used by monks, fashioned of antique, forged and polished iron, the head and foot adorned with thick filigrees of blossoming tulips enlaced with vine branches and leaves. Once this had been part of a balustrade of an old hostel's superb staircase.

For his table, he installed an antique praying-desk the inside of which could contain an urn and the outside a prayer book. Against the wall, opposite it, he placed a church pew surmounted by a tall dais with little benches carved out of solid wood. His church tapers were made of real wax, procured from a special house which catered exclusively to houses of worship, for Des Esseintes professed a sincere repugnance to gas, oil and ordinary candles, to all modern forms of illumination, so gaudy and brutal.

Before going to sleep in the morning, he would gaze, with his head on the pillows, at his El Greco whose barbaric color rebuked the smiling, yellow material and recalled it to a more serious tone. Then he could easily imagine himself living a hundred leagues removed from Paris, far from society, in cloistral security.

And, all in all, the illusion was not difficult, since he led an existence that approached the life of a monk. Thus he had the advantages of monasticism without the inconveniences of its vigorous discipline, its lack of service, its dirt, its promiscuity and its monotonous idleness. Just as he had transformed his cell into a comfortable chamber, so had he made his life normal, pleasant, surrounded by comforts, occupied and free.

Like a hermit he was ripe for isolation, since life harassed him and he no longer desired anything of it. Again like a monk, he was depressed and in the grip of an obsessing lassitude, seized with the need of self-communion and with a desire to have nothing in common with the profane who were, for him, the utilitarian and the imbecile.

Although he experienced no inclination for the state of grace, he felt a genuine sympathy for those souls immured in monasteries, persecuted by a vengeful society which can forgive neither the merited scorn with which it inspires them, nor the desire to expiate, to atone by long silences, for the ever growing shamelessness of its ridiculous or trifling gossipings.

Chapter 7

Ever since the night when he had evoked, for no apparent reason, a whole train of melancholy memories, pictures of his past life returned to Des Esseintes and gave him no peace.

He found himself unable to understand a single word of the books he read. He could not even receive impressions through his eyes. It seemed to him that his mind, saturated with literature and art, refused to absorb any more.

He lived within himself, nourished by his own substance, like some torpid creature which hibernates in caves. Solitude had reacted upon his brain like a narcotic. After having strained and enervated it, his mind had fallen victim to a sluggishness which annihilated his plans, broke his will power and invoked a cortège of vague reveries to which he passively submitted.

The confused medley of meditations on art and literature in which he had indulged since his isolation, as a dam to bar the current of old memories, had been rudely swept away, and the onrushing, irresistible wave crashed into the present and future, submerging everything beneath the blanket of the past, filling his mind with an immensity of sorrow, on whose surface floated, like futile wreckage, absurd trifles and dull episodes of his life.

The book he held in his hands fell to his knees. He abandoned himself to the mood which dominated him, watching the dead years of his life filled with so many disgusts and fears, move past. What a life he had lived! He thought of the evenings spent in society, the horse races, card parties, love affairs ordered in advance and served at the stroke of midnight, in his rose-colored boudoir! He recalled faces, expressions, vain words which obsessed him with the stubbornness of popular melodies which one cannot help humming, but which suddenly and inexplicably end by boring one.

This phase had not lasted long. His memory gave him respite and he plunged again into his Latin studies, so as to efface the impressions of such recollections.

But almost instantly the rushing force of his memories swept him into a second phase, that of his childhood, especially of the years spent at the school of the Fathers.

Although more remote, they were more positive and more indelibly stamped on his brain. The leafy park, the long walks, the flower beds, the benches—all the actual details of the monastery rose before him, here in his room.

The gardens filled and he heard the ringing cries of the students, mingling with the laughter of the professors as they played tennis, with their cassocks tucked up between their knees, or perhaps chatted under the trees with the youngsters, without any posturing or hauteur, as though they were companions of the same age.

He recalled the easy yoke of the monks who declined to administer punishment by inflicting the committment of five hundred or a thousand lines while the others were at play, being satisfied with making those delinquents prepare the lesson that had not been mastered, and most often simply having recourse to a gentle admonition. They surrounded the children with an active but gentle watch, seeking to please them, consenting to whatever expeditions they wished to take on Tuesdays, taking the occasion of every minor holiday not formally observed by the Church to add cakes and wine to the ordinary fare, and to entertain them with picnics. It was a paternal discipline whose success lay in the fact that they did not seek to domineer over the pupils, that they gossiped with them, treating them as men while showering them with the attentions paid a spoiled child.

In this manner, the monks succeeded in assuming a real influence over the youngsters; in molding, to some extent, the minds which they were cultivating; in directing them, in a sense; in instilling special ideas; in assuring the growth of their thoughts by insinuating, wheedling methods with which they continued to flatter them throughout their careers, taking pains not to lose sight of them in their later life, and by sending them affectionate letters like those which the Dominican Lacordaire so skillfully wrote to his former pupils of Sorrèze.

Des Esseintes took note of this system which had been so fruitlessly expended on him. His stubborn, captious and inquisitive character, disposed to controversies, had prevented him from being modelled by their discipline or subdued by their lessons. His scepticism had increased after he left the precincts of the college. His association with a legitimist, intolerant and shallow society, his conversations with unintelligent church wardens and abbots, whose blunders tore away the veil so subtly woven by the Jesuits, had still more fortified his spirit of independence and increased his scorn for any faith whatever.

He had deemed himself free of all bonds and constraints. Unlike most graduates of lycées or private schools, he had preserved a vivid memory of his college and of his masters. And now, as he considered these matters, he asked himself if the seeds sown until now on barren soil were not beginning to take root.

For several days, in fact, his soul had been strangely perturbed. At moments, he felt himself veering towards religion. Then, at the slightest approach of reason, his faith would dissolve. Yet he remained deeply troubled.

Analyzing himself, he was well aware that he would never possess a truly Christian spirit of humility and penitence. He knew without a doubt that he would never experience that moment of grace mentioned by Lacordaire, "when the last shaft of light penetrates the soul and unites the truths there lying dispersed." He never felt the need of mortification and of prayer, without which no conversion in possible, if one is to believe the majority of priests. He had no desire to implore a God whose forgiveness seemed most improbable. Yet the sympathy he felt for his old teachers lent him an interest in their works and doctrines. Those inimitable accents of conviction, those ardent voices of men of indubitably superior intelligence returned to him and led him to doubt his own mind and strength. Amid the solitude in which he lived, without new nourishment, without any fresh experiences, without any renovation of thought, without that exchange of sensations common to society, in this unnatural confinement in which he persisted, all the questionings forgotten during his stay in Paris were revived as active irritants. The reading of his beloved Latin works, almost all of them written by bishops and monks, had doubtless contributed to this crisis. Enveloped in a convent-like atmosphere, in a heady perfume of incense, his nervous brain had grown excitable. And by an association of ideas, these books had driven back the memories of his life as a young man, revealing in full light the years spent with the Fathers.

"There is no doubt about it," Des Esseintes mused, as he reasoned the matter and followed the progress of this introduction of the Jesuitic spirit into Fontenay. "Since my childhood, although unaware of it, I have had this leaven which has never fermented. The weakness I have always borne for religious subjects is perhaps a positive proof of it." But he sought to persuade himself to the contrary, disturbed at no longer being his own master. He searched for motives; it had required a struggle for him to abandon things sacerdotal, since the Church alone had treasured objects of art—the lost forms of past ages. Even in its wretched modern reproductions, she had preserved the contours of the gold and silver ornaments, the charm of chalices curving like petunias, and the charm of pyxes with their chaste sides; even in aluminum and imitation enamels and colored glasses, she had preserved the grace of vanished modes. In short, most of the precious objects now to be found in the Cluny museum, which have miraculously escaped the crude barbarism of the philistines, come from the ancient French abbeys. And just as the Church had preserved philosophy and history and letters from barbarism in the Middle Ages, so had she saved the plastic arts, bringing to our own days those marvelous fabrics and jewelries which the makers of sacred objects spoil to the best of their ability, without being able to destroy the originally exquisite form. It followed, then, that there was nothing surprising in his having bought these old trinkets, in his having, together with a number of other collectors, purchased such relics from the antique shops of Paris and the second-hand dealers of the provinces.

But these reasons he evoked in vain. He did not wholly succeed in convincing himself. He persisted in considering religion as a superb legend, a magnificent imposture. Yet, despite his convictions, his scepticism began to be shattered.

This was the singular fact he was obliged to face: he was less confident now than in childhood, when he had been directly under the influence of the Jesuits, when their instruction could not be shunned, when he was in their hands and belonged to them body and soul, without family ties, with no outside influence powerful enough to counteract their precepts. Moreover, they had inculcated in him a certain tendency towards the marvelous which, interned and exercised in the close quarters of his fixed ideas, had slowly and obscurely developed in his soul, until today it was blossoming in his solitude, affecting his spirit, regardless of arguments.

By examining the process of his reasoning, by seeking to unite its threads and to discover its sources and causes, he concluded that his previous mode of living was derived from the education he had received. Thus, his tendencies towards artificiality and his craving for eccentricity, were no more than the results of specious studies, spiritual refinements and quasi-theological speculations. They were, in the last analysis, ecstacies, aspirations towards an ideal, towards an unknown universe as desirable as that promised us by the Holy Scriptures.

He curbed his thoughts sharply and broke the thread of his reflections.

"Well!" he thought, vexed, "I am even more affected than I had imagined. Here am I arguing with myself like a very casuist!"

He was left pensive, agitated by a vague fear. Certainly, if Lacordaire's theory were sound, he had nothing to be afraid of, since the magic touch of conversion is not to be consummated in a moment. To bring about the explosion, the ground must be constantly and assiduously mined. But just as the romancers speak of the thunderclap of love, so do theologians also speak of the thunderclap of conversion. No one was safe, should one admit the truth of this doctrine. There was no longer any need of self-analysis, of paying heed to presentiments, of taking preventive measures. The psychology of mysticism was void. Things were so because they were so, and that was all.

"I am really becoming stupid," thought Des Esseintes. "The very fear of this malady will end by bringing it on, if this continues."

He partially succeeded in shaking off this influence. The memories of his life with the Jesuits waned, only to be replaced by other thoughts. He was entirely dominated by morbid abstractions. Despite himself, he thought of the contradictory interpretations of the dogmas, of the lost apostasies of Father Labbe, recorded in the works on the Decrees. Fragments of these schisms, scraps of these heresies which for centuries had divided the Churches of the Orient and the Occident, returned to him.

Here, Nestorius denied the title of "Mother of God" to the Virgin because, in the mystery of the Incarnation, it was not God but rather a human being she had nourished in her womb; there, Eutyches declared that Christ's image could not resemble that of other men, since divinity had chosen to dwell in his body and had consequently entirely altered the form of everything. Other quibblers maintained that the Redeemer had had no body at all and that this expression of the holy books must be taken figuratively, while Tertullian put forth his famous, semi-materialistic axiom: "Only that which is not, has no body; everything which is, has a body fitting it." Finally, this ancient question, debated for years, demanded an answer: was Christ hanged on the cross, or was it the Trinity which had suffered as one in its triple hypostasis, on the cross at Calvary? And mechanically, like a lesson long ago learned, he proposed the questions to himself and answered them.

For several days his brain was a swarm of paradoxes, subtleties and hair-splittings, a skein of rules as complicated as the articles of the codes that involved the sense of everything, indulged in puns and ended in a most tenuous and singular celestial jurisprudence. The abstract side vanished, in its turn, and under the influence of the Gustave Moreau paintings of the wall, yielded to a concrete succession of pictures.

Before him he saw marching a procession of prelates. The archimandrites and patriarchs, their white beards waving during the reading of the prayers, lifted golden arms to bless kneeling throngs. He saw silent files of penitents marching into dim crypts. Before him rose vast cathedrals where white monks intoned from pulpits. Just as De Quincey, having taken a dose of opium and uttered the word "Consul Romanus," evoked entire pages of Livius, and beheld the solemn advance of the consuls and the magnificent, pompous march of the Roman armies, so he, at a theological expression, paused breathless as he viewed the onrush of penitents and the churchly apparitions which detached themselves from the glowing depths of the basilica. These scenes held him enchanted. They moved from age to age, culminating in the modern religious ceremonies, bathing his soul in a tender, mournful infinity of music.

On this plane, no reasonings were necessary; there were no further contests to be endured. He had an indescribable impression of respect and fear. His artistic sense was conquered by the skillfully calculated Catholic rituals. His nerves quivered at these memories. Then, in sudden rebellion, in a sudden reversion, monstrous ideas were born in him, fancies concerning those sacrileges warned against by the manual of the Father confessors, of the scandalous, impure desecration of holy water and sacred oil. The Demon, a powerful rival, now stood against an omnipotent God. A frightful grandeur seemed to Des Esseintes to emanate from a crime committed in church by a believer bent, with blasphemously horrible glee and sadistic joy, over such revered objects, covering them with outrages and saturating them in opprobrium.

Before him were conjured up the madnesses of magic, of the black mass, of the witches' revels, of terrors of possessions and of exorcisms. He reached the point where he wondered if he were not committing a sacrilege in possessing objects which had once been consecrated: the Church canons, chasubles and pyx covers. And this idea of a state of sin imparted to him a mixed sensation of pride and relief. The pleasures of sacrilege were unravelled from the skein of this idea, but these were debatable sacrileges, in any case, and hardly serious, since he really loved these objects and did not pollute them by misuse. In this wise he lulled himself with prudent and cowardly thoughts, the caution of his soul forbidding obvious crimes and depriving him of the courage necessary to the consummation of frightful and deliberate sins.

Little by little this tendency to ineffectual quibbling disappeared. In his mind's eye he saw the panorama of the Church with its hereditary influence on humanity through the centuries. He imagined it as imposing and suffering, emphasizing to man the horror of life, the infelicity of man's destiny; preaching patience, penitence and the spirit of sacrifice; seeking to heal wounds, while it displayed the bleeding wounds of Christ; bespeaking divine privileges; promising the richest part of paradise to the afflicted; exhorting humanity to suffer and to render to God, like a holocaust, its trials and offenses, its vicissitudes and pains. Thus the Church grew truly eloquent, the beneficent mother of the oppressed, the eternal menace of oppressors and despots.

Here, Des Esseintes was on firm ground. He was thoroughly satisfied with this admission of social ordure, but he revolted against the vague hope of remedy in the beyond. Schopenhauer was more true. His doctrine and that of the Church started from common premises. He, too, based his system on the vileness of the world; he, too, like the author of the Imitation of Christ, uttered that grievous outcry: "Truly life on earth is wretched." He, also, preached the nothingness of life, the advantages of solitude, and warned humanity that no matter what it does, in whatever direction it may turn, it must remain wretched, the poor by reason of the sufferings entailed by want, the rich by reason of the unconquerable weariness engendered by abundance; but this philosophy promised no universal remedies, did not entice one with false hopes, so as to minimize the inevitable evils of life.

He did not affirm the revolting conception of original sin, nor did he feel inclined to argue that it is a beneficent God who protects the worthless and wicked, rains misfortunes on children, stultifies the aged and afflicts the innocent. He did not exalt the virtues of a Providence which has invented that useless, incomprehensible, unjust and senseless abomination, physical suffering. Far from seeking to justify, as does the Church, the necessity of torments and afflictions, he cried, in his outraged pity: "If a God has made this world, I should not wish to be that God. The world's wretchedness would rend my heart."

Ah! Schopenhauer alone was right. Compared with these treatises of spiritual hygiene, of what avail were the evangelical pharmacopœias? He did not claim to cure anything, and he offered no alleviation to the sick. But his theory of pessimism was, in the end, the great consoler of choice intellects and lofty souls. He revealed society as it is, asserted woman's inherent stupidity, indicated the safest course, preserved you from disillusionment by warning you to restrain hopes as much as possible, to refuse to yield to their allurement, to deem yourself fortunate, finally, if they did not come toppling about your ears at some unexpected moment.

Traversing the same path as the Imitation, this theory, too, ended in similar highways of resignation and indifference, but without going astray in mysterious labyrinths and remote roads.

But if this resignation, which was obviously the only outcome of the deplorable condition of things and their irremediability, was open to the spiritually rich, it was all the more difficult of approach to the poor whose passions and cravings were more easily satisfied by the benefits of religion.

These reflections relieved Des Esseintes of a heavy burden. The aphorisms of the great German calmed his excited thoughts, and the points of contact in these two doctrines helped him to correlate them; and he could never forget that poignant and poetic Catholicism in which he had bathed, and whose essence he had long ago absorbed.

These reversions to religion, these intimations of faith tormented him particularly since the changes that had lately taken place in his health. Their progress coincided with that of his recent nervous disorders.

He had been tortured since his youth by inexplicable aversions, by shudderings which chilled his spine and made him grit his teeth, as, for example, when he saw a girl wringing wet linen. These reactions had long persisted. Even now he suffered poignantly when he heard the tearing of cloth, the rubbing of a finger against a piece of chalk, or a hand touching a bit of moire.

The excesses of his youthful life, the exaggerated tension of his mind had strangely aggravated his earliest nervous disorder, and had thinned the already impoverished blood of his race. In Paris, he had been compelled to submit to hydrotherapic treatments for his trembling fingers, frightful pains, neuralgic strokes which cut his face in two, drummed maddeningly against his temples, pricked his eyelids agonizingly and induced a nausea which could be dispelled only by lying flat on his back in the dark.

These afflictions had gradually disappeared, thanks to a more regulated and sane mode of living. They now returned in another form, attacking his whole body. The pains left his head, but affected his inflated stomach. His entrails seemed pierced by hot bars of iron. A nervous cough racked him at regular intervals, awakening and almost strangling him in his bed. Then his appetite forsook him; gaseous, hot acids and dry heats coursed through his stomach. He grew swollen, was choked for breath, and could not endure his clothes after each attempt at eating.

He shunned alcoholic beverages, coffee and tea, and drank only milk. And he took recourse to baths of cold water and dosed himself with assafœtida, valerian and quinine. He even felt a desire to go out, and strolled about the country when the rainy days came to make it desolate and still. He obliged himself to take exercise. As a last resort, he temporarily abandoned his books and, corroded with ennui, determined to make his listless life tolerable by realizing a project he had long deferred through laziness and a dislike of change, since his installment at Fontenay.

Being no longer able to intoxicate himself with the felicities of style, with the delicious witchery of the rare epithet which, while remaining precise, yet opens to the imagination of the initiate infinite and distant vistas, he determined to give the finishing touches to the decorations of his home. He would procure precious hot-house flowers and thus permit himself a material occupation which might distract him, calm his nerves and rest his brain. He also hoped that the sight of their strange and splendid nuances would in some degree atone for the fanciful and genuine colors of style which he was for the time to lose from his literary diet.

Chapter 8

He had always been passionately fond of flowers, but during his residence at Jutigny, that love had been lavished upon flowers of all sorts; he had never cultivated distinctions and discriminations in regard to them. Now his taste in this direction had grown refined and self-conscious.

For a long time he had scorned the popular plants which grow in flat baskets, in watered pots, under green awnings or under the red parasols of Parisian markets.

Simultaneous with the refinement of his literary taste and his preoccupations with art, which permitted him to be content only in the presence of choice creations, distilled by subtly troubled brains, and simultaneous with the weariness he began to feel in the presence of popular ideas, his love for flowers had grown purged of all impurities and lees, and had become clarified.

He compared a florist's shop to a microcosm wherein all the categories of society are represented. Here are poor common flowers, the kind found in hovels, which are truly at home only when resting on ledges of garret windows, their roots thrust into milk bottles and old pans, like the gilly-flower for example.

And one also finds stupid and pretentious flowers like the rose which belongs in the porcelain flowerpots painted by young girls.

Then, there are flowers of noble lineage like the orchid, so delicate and charming, at once cold and palpitating, exotic flowers exiled in the heated glass palaces of Paris, princesses of the vegetable kingdom living in solitude, having absolutely nothing in common with the street plants and other bourgeois flora.

He permitted himself to feel a certain interest and pity only for the popular flowers enfeebled by their nearness to the odors of sinks and drains in the poor quarters. In revenge he detested the bouquets harmonizing with the cream and gold rooms of pretentious houses. For the joy of his eyes he reserved those distinguished, rare blooms which had been brought from distant lands and whose lives were sustained by artful devices under artificial equators.

But this very choice, this predilection for the conservatory plants had itself changed under the influence of his mode of thought. Formerly, during his Parisian days, his love for artificiality had led him to abandon real flowers and to use in their place replicas faithfully executed by means of the miracles performed with India rubber and wire, calico and taffeta, paper and silk. He was the possessor of a marvelous collection of tropical plants, the result of the labors of skilful artists who knew how to follow nature and recreate her step by step, taking the flower as a bud, leading it to its full development, even imitating its decline, reaching such a point of perfection as to convey every nuance—the most fugitive expressions of the flower when it opens at dawn and closes at evening, observing the appearance of the petals curled by the wind or rumpled by the rain, applying dew drops of gum on its matutinal corollas; shaping it in full bloom, when the branches bend under the burden of their sap, or showing the dried stem and shrivelled cupules, when calyxes are thrown off and leaves fall to the ground.

This wonderful art had held him entranced for a long while, but now he was dreaming of another experiment.

He wished to go one step beyond. Instead of artificial flowers imitating real flowers, natural flowers should mimic the artificial ones.

He directed his ideas to this end and had not to seek long or go far, since his house lay in the very heart of a famous horticultural region. He visited the conservatories of the Avenue de Chatillon and of the Aunay valley, and returned exhausted, his purse empty, astonished at the strange forms of vegetation he had seen, thinking of nothing but the species he had acquired and continually haunted by memories of magnificent and fantastic plants.

The flowers came several days later.

Des Esseintes holding a list in his hands, verified each one of his purchases. The gardeners from their wagons brought a collection of caladiums which sustained enormous heartshaped leaves on turgid hairy stalks; while preserving an air of relationship with its neighbor, no one leaf repeated the same pattern.

Others were equally extraordinary. The roses like the Virginale seemed cut out of varnished cloth or oil-silks; the white ones, like the Albano, appeared to have been cut out of an ox's transparent pleura, or the diaphanous bladder of a pig. Some, particularly the Madame Mame, imitated zinc and parodied pieces of stamped metal having a hue of emperor green, stained by drops of oil paint and by spots of white and red lead; others like the Bosphorous, gave the illusion of a starched calico in crimson and myrtle green; still others, like the Aurora Borealis, displayed leaves having the color of raw meat, streaked with purple sides, violet fibrils, tumefied leaves from which oozed blue wine and blood.

The Albano and the Aurora sounded the two extreme notes of temperament, the apoplexy and chlorosis of this plant.

The gardeners brought still other varieties which had the appearance of artificial skin ridged with false veins, and most of them looked as though consumed by syphilis and leprosy, for they exhibited livid surfaces of flesh veined with scarlet rash and damasked with eruptions. Some had the deep red hue of scars that have just closed or the dark tint of incipient scabs. Others were marked with matter raised by scaldings. There were forms which exhibited shaggy skins hollowed by ulcers and relieved by cankers. And a few appeared embossed with wounds, covered with black mercurial hog lard, with green unguents of belladonna smeared with grains of dust and the yellow micas of iodoforme.

Collected in his home, these flowers seemed to Des Esseintes more monstrous than when he had beheld them, confused with others among the glass rooms of the conservatory.

"Sapristi!" he exclaimed enthusiastically.

A new plant, modelled like the Caladiums, the Alocasia Metallica, excited him even more. It was coated with a layer of bronze green on which glanced silver reflections. It was the masterpiece of artificiality. It could be called a piece of stove pipe, cut by a chimney-maker into the form of a pike head.

The men next brought clusters of leaves, lozenge-like in shape and bottle-green in color. In the center rose a rod at whose end a varnished ace of hearts swayed. As though meaning to defy all conceivable forms of plants, a fleshy stalk climbed through the heart of this intense vermilion ace—a stalk that in some specimens was straight, in others showed ringlets like a pig's tail.

It was the Anthurium, an aroid recently imported into France from Columbia; a variety of that family to which also belonged an Amorphophallus, a Cochin China plant with leaves shaped like fish-knives, with long dark stems seamed with gashes, like lambs flecked with black.

Des Esseintes exulted.

They brought a new batch of monstrosities from the wagon: Echinopses, issuing from padded compresses with rose-colored flowers that looked like the pitiful stumps; gaping Nidularia revealing skinless foundations in steel plates; Tillandsia Lindeni, the color of wine must, with jagged scrapers; Cypripedia, with complicated contours, a crazy piece of work seemingly designed by a crazy inventor. They looked like sabots or like a lady's work-table on which lies a human tongue with taut filaments, such as one sees designed on the illustrated pages of works treating of the diseases of the throat and mouth; two little side-pieces, of a red jujube color, which appeared to have been borrowed from a child's toy mill completed this singular collection of a tongue's underside with the color of slate and wine lees, and of a glossy pocket from whose lining oozed a viscous glue.

He could not remove his eyes from this unnatural orchid which had been brought from India. Then the gardeners, impatient at his procrastinations, themselves began to read the labels fastened to the pots they were carrying in.

Bewildered, Des Esseintes looked on and listened to the cacophonous sounds of the names: the Encephalartos horridus, a gigantic iron rust-colored artichoke, like those put on portals of chateaux to foil wall climbers; the Cocos Micania, a sort of notched and slender palm surrounded by tall leaves resembling paddles and oars; the Zamia Lehmanni, an immense pineapple, a wondrous Chester leaf, planted in sweet-heather soil, its top bristling with barbed javelins and jagged arrows; the Cibotium Spectabile, surpassing the others by the craziness of its structure, hurling a defiance to revery, as it darted, through the palmated foliage, an enormous orang-outang tail, a hairy dark tail whose end was twisted into the shape of a bishop's cross.

But he gave little heed, for he was impatiently awaiting the series of plants which most bewitched him, the vegetable ghouls, the carnivorous plants; the Antilles Fly-Trap, with its shaggy border, secreting a digestive liquid, armed with crooked prickles coiling around each other, forming a grating about the imprisoned insect; the Drosera of the peat-bogs, provided with glandular hair; the Sarracena and the Cephalothus, opening greedy horns capable of digesting and absorbing real meat; lastly, the Nepenthes, whose capricious appearance transcends all limits of eccentric forms.

He never wearied of turning in his hands the pot in which this floral extravagance stirred. It imitated the gum-tree whose long leaf of dark metallic green it possessed, but it differed in that a green string hung from the end of its leaf, an umbilic cord supporting a greenish urn, streaked with jasper, a sort of German porcelain pipe, a strange bird's nest which tranquilly swung about, revealing an interior covered with hair.

"This is really something worth while," Des Esseintes murmured.

He was forced to tear himself away, for the gardeners, anxious to leave, were emptying the wagons of their contents and depositing, without any semblance of order, the tuberous Begonias and black Crotons stained like sheet iron with Saturn red.

Then he perceived that one name still remained on his list. It was the Cattleya of New Granada. On it was designed a little winged bell of a faded lilac, an almost dead mauve. He approached, placed his nose above the plant and quickly recoiled. It exhaled an odor of toy boxes of painted pine; it recalled the horrors of a New Year's Day.

He felt that he would do well to mistrust it and he almost regretted having admitted, among the scentless plants, this orchid which evoked the most disagreeable memories.

As soon as he was alone his gaze took in this vegetable tide which foamed in the vestibule. Intermingled with each other, they crossed their swords, their krisses and stanchions, taking on a resemblance to a green pile of arms, above which, like barbaric penons, floated flowers with hard dazzling colors.

The air of the room grew rarefied. Then, in the shadowy dimness of a corner, near the floor, a white soft light crept.

He approached and perceived that the phenomenon came from the Rhizomorphes which threw out these night-lamp gleams while respiring.

"These plants are amazing," he reflected. Then he drew back to let his eye encompass the whole collection at a glance. His purpose was achieved. Not one single specimen seemed real; the cloth, paper, porcelain and metal seemed to have been loaned by man to nature to enable her to create her monstrosities. When unable to imitate man's handiwork, nature had been reduced to copying the inner membranes of animals, to borrowing the vivid tints of their rotting flesh, their magnificent corruptions.

"All is syphilis," thought Des Esseintes, his eye riveted upon the horrible streaked stainings of the Caladium plants caressed by a ray of light. And he beheld a sudden vision of humanity consumed through the centuries by the virus of this disease. Since the world's beginnings, every single creature had, from sire to son, transmitted the imperishable heritage, the eternal malady which has ravaged man's ancestors and whose effects are visible even in the bones of old fossils that have been exhumed.

The disease had swept on through the centuries gaining momentum. It even raged today, concealed in obscure sufferings, dissimulated under symptoms of headaches and bronchitis, hysterics and gout. It crept to the surface from time to time, preferably attacking the ill-nourished and the poverty stricken, spotting faces with gold pieces, ironically decorating the faces of poor wretches, stamping the mark of money on their skins to aggravate their unhappiness.

And here on the colored leaves of the plants it was resurgent in its original splendor.

"It is true," pursued Des Esseintes, returning to the course of reasoning he had momentarily abandoned, "it is true that most often nature, left alone, is incapable of begetting such perverse and sickly specimens. She furnishes the original substance, the germ and the earth, the nourishing womb and the elements of the plant which man then sets up, models, paints, and sculpts as he wills. Limited, stubborn and formless though she be, nature has at last been subjected and her master has succeeded in changing, through chemical reaction, the earth's substances, in using combinations which had been long matured, cross-fertilization processes long prepared, in making use of slips and graftings, and man now forces differently colored flowers in the same species, invests new tones for her, modifies to his will the long-standing form of her plants, polishes the rough clods, puts an end to the period of botch work, places his stamp on them, imposes on them the mark of his own unique art."

"It cannot be gainsaid," he thought, resuming his reflections, "that man in several years is able to effect a selection which slothful nature can produce only after centuries. Decidedly the horticulturists are the real artists nowadays."

He was a little tired and he felt stifled in this atmosphere of crowded plants. The promenades he had taken during the last few days had exhausted him. The transition had been too sudden from the tepid atmosphere of his room to the out-of-doors, from the placid tranquillity of a reclusive life to an active one. He left the vestibule and stretched out on his bed to rest, but, absorbed by this new fancy of his, his mind, even in his sleep, could not lessen its tension and he was soon wandering among the gloomy insanities of a nightmare.

He found himself in the center of a walk, in the heart of the wood; twilight had fallen. He was strolling by the side of a woman whom he had never seen before. She was emaciated and had flaxen hair, a bulldog face, freckles on her cheeks, crooked teeth projecting under a flat nose. She wore a nurse's white apron, a long neckerchief, torn in strips on her bosom; half-shoes like those worn by Prussian soldiers and a black bonnet adorned with frillings and trimmed with a rosette.

There was a foreign look about her, like that of a mountebank at a fair.

He asked himself who the woman could be; he felt that she had long been an intimate part of his life; vainly he sought her origin, her name, her profession, her reason for being. No recollection of this liaison, which was inexplicable and yet positive, rewarded him.

He was searching his past for a clue, when a strange figure suddenly appeared on horse-back before them, trotting about for a moment and then turning around in its saddle. Des Esseintes' heart almost stopped beating and he stood riveted to the spot with horror. He nearly fainted. This enigmatic, sexless figure was green; through her violet eyelids the eyes were terrible in their cold blue; pimples surrounded her mouth; horribly emaciated, skeleton arms bared to the elbows issued from ragged tattered sleeves and trembled feverishly; and the skinny legs shivered in shoes that were several sizes too large.

The ghastly eyes were fixed on Des Esseintes, penetrating him, freezing his very marrow; wilder than ever, the bulldog woman threw herself at him and commenced to howl like a dog at the killing, her head hanging on her rigid neck.

Suddenly he understood the meaning of the frightful vision. Before him was the image of Syphilis.

Pursued by fear and quite beside himself, he sped down a pathway at top speed and gained a pavillion standing among the laburnums to the left, where he fell into a chair, in the passage way.

After a few moments, when he was beginning to recover his breath, the sound of sobbing made him lift his head. The bulldog woman was in front of him and, grotesque and woeful, while warm tears fell from her eyes, she told him that she had lost her teeth in her flight. As she spoke she drew clay pipes from the pocket of her nurse's apron, breaking them and shoving pieces of the stems into the hollows of her gums.

"But she is really absurd," Des Esseintes told himself. "These stems will never stick." And, as a matter of fact, they dropped out one after another.

At this moment were heard the galloping sounds of an approaching horse. A fearful terror pierced Des Esseintes. His limbs gave way. The galloping grew louder. Despair brought him sharply to his senses. He threw himself upon the woman who was stamping on the pipe bowls, entreating her to be silent, not to give notice of their presence by the sound of her shoes. She writhed and struggled in his grip; he led her to the end of the corridor, strangling her to prevent her from crying out. Suddenly he noticed the door of a coffee house, with green Venetian shutters. It was unlocked; he pushed it, rushed in headlong and then paused.

Before him, in the center of a vast glade, huge white pierrots were leaping rabbit-like under the rays of the moon.

Tears of discouragement welled to his eyes; never, no never would he succeed in crossing the threshold. "I shall be crushed," he thought. And as though to justify his fears, the ranks of tall pierrots swarmed and multiplied; their somersaults now covered the entire horizon, the whole sky on which they landed now on their heads, now on their feet.

Then the hoof beats paused. He was in the passage, behind a round skylight. More dead than alive, Des Esseintes turned about and through the round window beheld projecting erect ears, yellow teeth, nostrils from which breathed two jets of vapor smelling of phenol.

He sank to the ground, renouncing all ideas of flight or of resistance. He closed his eyes so as not to behold the horrible gaze of Syphilis which penetrated through the wall, which even pierced his closed lids, which he felt gliding over his moist spine, over his body whose hair bristled in pools of cold sweat. He waited for the worst and even hoped for the coup de grâce to end everything. A moment which seemed to last a century passed. Shuddering, he opened his eyes. Everything had vanished. Without any transition, as though by some stage device, a frightful mineral landscape receded into the distance, a wan, dead, waste, gullied landscape. A light illumined this desolate site, a peaceful white light that recalled gleams of phosphorus dissolved in oil.

Something that stirred on the ground became a deathly pale, nude woman whose feet were covered with green silk stockings.

He contemplated her with curiosity. As though frizzed by overheated irons, her hair curled, becoming straight again at the end; her distended nostrils were the color of roast veal. Her eyes were desirous, and she called to him in low tones.

He had no time to answer, for already the woman was changing. Flamboyant colors passed and repassed in her eyes. Her lips were stained with a furious Anthurium red. The nipples of her breasts flashed, painted like two pods of red pepper.

A sudden intuition came to him. "It is the Flower," he said. And his reasoning mania persisted in his nightmare.

Then he observed the frightful irritation of the breasts and mouth, discovered spots of bister and copper on the skin of her body, and recoiled bewildered. But the woman's eyes fascinated him and he advanced slowly, attempting to thrust his heels into the earth so as not to move, letting himself fall, and yet lifting himself to reach her. Just as he touched her, the dark Amorphophalli leaped up from all sides and thrust their leaves into his abdomen which rose and fell like a sea. He had broken all the plants, experiencing a limitless disgust in seeing these warm, firm stems stirring in his hands. Suddenly the detested plants had disappeared and two arms sought to enlace him. A terrible anguish made his heart beat furiously, for the eyes, the horrible eyes of the woman, had become a clear, cold and terrible blue. He made a superhuman effort to free himself from her embrace, but she held him with an irresistible movement. He beheld the wild Nidularium which yawned, bleeding, in steel plates.

With his body he touched the hideous wound of this plant. He felt himself dying, awoke with a start, suffocating, frozen, mad with fear and sighing: "Ah! thank God, it was but a dream!"

Chapter 9

These nightmares attacked him repeatedly. He was afraid to fall asleep. For hours he remained stretched on his bed, now a prey to feverish and agitated wakefulness, now in the grip of oppressive dreams in which he tumbled down flights of stairs and felt himself sinking, powerless, into abysmal depths.

His nervous attacks, which had abated for several days, became acute, more violent and obstinate than ever, unearthing new tortures.

The bed covers tormented him. He stifled under the sheets, his body smarted and tingled as though stung by swarms of insects. These symptoms were augmented by a dull pain in his jaws and a throbbing in his temples which seemed to be gripped in a vise.

His alarm increased; but unfortunately the means of subduing the inexorable malady were not at hand. He had unsuccessfully sought to install a hydropathic apparatus in his dressing room. But the impossibility of forcing water to the height on which his house was perched, and the difficulty of procuring water even in the village where the fountains functioned sparingly and only at certain hours of the day, caused him to renounce the project. Since he could not have floods of water playing on him from the nozzle of a hose, (the only efficacious means of overcoming his insomnia and calming his nerves through its action on his spinal column) he was reduced to brief sprays or to mere cold baths, followed by energetic massages applied by his servant with the aid of a horse-hair glove.

But these measures failed to stem the march of his nervous disorder. At best they afforded him a few hours' relief, dearly paid for by the return of the attacks in an even more virulent form.

His ennui passed all bounds. His pleasure in the possession of his wonderful flowers was exhausted. Their textures and nuances palled on him. Besides, despite the care he lavished on them, most of his plants drooped. He had them removed from his rooms, but in his state of extreme excitability, their very absence exasperated him, for his eyes were pained by the void.

To while away the interminable hours, he had recourse to his portfolios of prints, and arranged his Goyas. The first impressions of certain plates of the Caprices, recognizable as proofs by their reddish hues, which he had bought at auction at a high price, comforted him, and he lost himself in them, following the painter's fantasies, distracted by his vertiginous scenes, his witches astride on cats, his women striving to pluck out the teeth of a hanged man, his bandits, his succubi, his demons and dwarfs.

Then he examined his other series of etchings and aquatints, his Proverbs with their macabre horror, his war subjects with their wild rage, finally his plate of the Garot, of which he cherished a marvelous trial proof, printed on heavy water-marked paper, unmounted.

Goya's savage verve and keenly fanciful talent delighted him, but the universal admiration his works had won nevertheless estranged him slightly. And for years he had refused to frame them for fear that the first blundering fool who caught sight of them might deem it necessary to fly into banal and facile raptures before them.

The same applied to his Rembrandts which he examined from time to time, half secretly; and if it be true that the loveliest tune imaginable becomes vulgar and insupportable as soon as the public begins to hum it and the hurdy-gurdies make it their own, the work of art which does not remain indifferent to the spurious artists, which is not contested by fools, and which is not satisfied with awakening the enthusiasm of the few, by this very fact becomes profaned, trite, almost repulsive to the initiate.

This promiscuity in admiration, furthermore, was one of the greatest sources of regret in his life. Incomprehensible successes had forever spoiled for him many pictures and books once cherished and dear. Approved by the mob, they began to reveal imperceptible defects to him, and he rejected them, wondering meanwhile if his perceptions were not growing blunted.

He closed his portfolios and, completely disconcerted, again plunged into melancholy. To divert the current of his thoughts and cool his brain, he sought books that would soothe him and turned to the romances of Dickens, those charming novels which are so satisfying to invalids and convalescents who might grow fatigued by works of a more profound and vigorous nature.

But they produced an effect contrary to his expectations. These chaste lovers, these protesting heroines garbed to the neck, loved among the stars, confined themselves to lowered eyes and blushes, wept tears of joy and clasped hands—an exaggeration of purity which threw him into an opposite excess. By the law of contrast, he leaped from one extreme to the other, let his imagination dwell on vibrant scenes between human lovers, and mused on their sensual kisses and passionate embraces.

His mind wandered off from his book to worlds far removed from the English prude: to wanton peccadilloes and salacious practices condemned by the Church. He grew excited. The impotence of his mind and body which he had supposed final, vanished. Solitude again acted on his disordered nerves; he was once more obsessed, not by religion itself, but by the acts and sins it forbids, by the subject of all its obsecrations and threats. The carnal side, atrophied for months, which had been stirred by the enervation of his pious readings, then brought to a crisis by the English cant, came to the surface. His stimulated senses carried him back to the past and he wallowed in memories of his old sin.

He rose and pensively opened a little box of vermeil with a lid of aventurine.

It was filled with violet bonbons. He took one up and pressed it between his fingers, thinking of the strange properties of this sugary, frosted sweetmeat. When his virility had been impaired, when the thought of woman had roused in him no sharp regret or desire, he had only to put one in his mouth, let it melt, and almost at once it induced misty, languishing memories, infinitely tender.

These bonbons invented by Siraudin and bearing the ridiculous name of "Perles des Pyrénées" were each a drop of sarcanthus perfume, a drop of feminine essence crystallized in a morsel of sugar. They penetrated the papillæ of the tongue, recalling the very savor of voluptuous kisses.

Usually he smiled as he inhaled this love aroma, this shadow of a caress which for a moment restored the delights of women he had once adored. Today they were not merely suggestive, they no longer served as a delicate hint of his distant riotous past. They were become powerful, thrusting aside the veils, exposing before his eyes the importunate, corporeal and brutal reality.

At the head of the procession of mistresses whom the fragrance of the bonbons helped to place in bold relief, one paused, displaying long white teeth, a satiny rose skin, a snub nose, mouse-colored eyes, and close-cropped blond hair.

This was Miss Urania, an American, with a vigorous body, sinewy limbs, muscles of steel and arms of iron.

She had been one of the most celebrated acrobats of the Circus.

Des Esseintes had watched her attentively through many long evenings. At first, she had seemed to him what she really was, a strong and beautiful woman, but the desire to know her never troubled him. She possessed nothing to recommend her in the eyes of a blasé man, and yet he returned to the Circus, allured by he knew not what, importuned by a sentiment difficult to define.

Gradually, as he watched her, a fantastic idea seized him. Her graceful antics and arch feminine ways receded to the background of his mind, replaced by her power and strength which had for him all the charm of masculinity. Compared with her, Des Esseintes seemed to himself a frail, effeminate creature, and he began to desire her as ardently as an anæmic young girl might desire some loutish Hercules whose arms could crush her in a strong embrace.

One evening he finally decided to communicate with her and dispatched one of the attendants on this errand. Miss Urania deemed it necessary not to yield before a preliminary courtship; but she showed herself amenable, as it was common gossip that Des Esseintes was rich and that his name was instrumental in establishing women.

But as soon as his wishes were granted, his disappointment surpassed any he had yet experienced. He had persuaded himself that the American woman would be as bestial and stupid as a wrestler at a county fair, and instead her stupidity was of an altogether feminine nature. Certainly, she lacked education and tact, had neither good sense nor wit, and displayed an animal voracity at table, but she possessed all the childish traits of a woman. Her manner and speech were coquettish and affected, those of a silly, scandal-loving young girl. There was absolutely nothing masculine about her.

Furthermore, she was withdrawn and puritanical in her embraces, displaying none of the brute force he had dreaded yet longed for, and she was subject to none of the perturbations of his sex.

Des Esseintes inevitably returned to the masculine rôle he had momentarily abandoned.

His impression of femininity, weakness, need of protection, of fear even, disappeared. The illusion was no longer possible! Miss Urania was an ordinary mistress, in no wise justifying the cerebral curiosity she had at first awakened in him.

Although the charm of her firm skin and magnificent beauty had at first astonished and captivated Des Esseintes, he lost no time in terminating this liaison, for his impotence was prematurely hastened by the frozen and prudish caresses of this woman.

And yet she was the first of all the women he had loved, now flitting through his revery, to stand out. But if she was more strongly imprinted on his memory than a host of others whose allurements had been less spurious and more seductive, the reason must be ascribed to her healthy animalism, to her exuberance which contrasted so strikingly with the perfumed anæmia of the others, a faint suggestion of which he found in the delicate Siraudin bonbon.

Miss Urania haunted him by reason of her very difference, but almost instantly, offended by the intrusion of this natural, crude aroma, the antithesis of the scented confection, Des Esseintes returned to more civilized exhalations and his thoughts reverted to his other mistresses. They pressed upon him in a throng; but above them all rose a woman whose startling talents had satisfied him for months.

She was a little, slender brunette, with black eyes and burnished hair parted on one side and sleeked down over her head. He had known her in a café where she gave ventriloqual performances.

Before the amazed patrons, she caused her tiny cardboard figures, placed near each other on chairs, to talk; she conversed with the animated mannikins while flies buzzed around the chandeliers. Then one heard the rustling of the tense audience, surprised to find itself seated and instinctively recoiling when they heard the rumbling of imaginary carriages.

Des Esseintes had been fascinated. He lost no time in winning over the ventriloquist, tempting her with large sums of money. She delighted him by the very contrast she exhibited to the American woman. This brunette used strong perfumes and burned like a crater. Despite all her blandishments, Des Esseintes wearied of her in a few short hours. But this did not prevent him from letting himself be fleeced, for the phenomenon of the ventriloquist attracted him more than did the charms of the mistress.

Certain plans he had long pondered upon ripened, and he decided to bring them to fruition.

One evening he ordered a tiny sphinx brought in—a sphinx carved from black marble and resting in the classic pose with outstretched paws and erect head. He also purchased a chimera of polychrome clay; it brandished its mane of hair, and its sides resembled a pair of bellows. These two images he placed in a corner of the room. Then he extinguished the lamps, permitting the glowing embers to throw a dim light around the room and to magnify the objects which were almost immersed in gloom.

Then he stretched out on a couch beside the woman whose motionless figure was touched by the ember gleams, and waited.

With strange intonations that he had long and patiently taught her, she animated the two monsters; she did not even move her lips, she did not even glance in their direction.

And in the silence followed the marvelous dialogue of the Chimera and the Sphinx; it was recited in deep guttural tones which were at first raucous, then turned shrill and unearthly.

"Here, Chimera, pause!"

"Never!"

Lulled by the admirable prose of Flaubert, he listened; he panted and shivering sensations raced through his frame, when the Chimera uttered the magical and solemn phrase:

"New perfumes I seek, stranger flowers I seek, pleasures not yet discovered."

Ah! it was to him that this voice, mysterious as an incantation, spoke; it was to him that this voice recounted her feverish agitation for the unknown, her insatiable ideals, her imperative need to escape from the horrible reality of existence, to leap beyond the confines of thought, to grope towards the mists of elusive, unattainable art. The poignant tragedy of his past failures rent his heart. Gently he clasped the silent woman at his side, he sought refuge in her nearness, like a child who is inconsolable; he was blind to the sulkiness of the comedienne obliged to perform off-scene, in her leisure moments, far from the spotlight.

Their liaison continued, but his spells of exhaustion soon became acute. His brain no longer sufficed to stimulate his benumbed body. No longer did his nerves obey his will; and now the crazy whims of dotards dominated him. Terrified by the approach of a disastrous weakness in the presence of his mistress, he resorted to fear—that oldest, most efficacious of excitants.

A hoarse voice from behind the door would exclaim, while he held the woman in his arms: "Open the door, woman, I know you're in there, and with whom. Just wait, wait!" Instantly, like a libertine stirred by fear of discovery in the open, he recovered his strength and hurled himself madly upon the ventriloquist whose voice continued to bluster outside the room. In this wise he experienced the pleasures of a panic-stricken person.

But this state, unfortunately, did not last long, and despite the sums he paid her, the ventriloquist parted to offer herself to someone less exigent and less complex.

He had regretted her defection, and now, recalling her, the other women seemed insipid, their childish graces and monotonous coquetry disgusting him.

In the ferment of his disordered brain, he delighted in mingling with these recollections of his past, other more gloomy pleasures, as theology qualifies the evocation of past, disgraceful acts. With the physical visions he mingled spiritual ardors brought into play and motivated by his old readings of the casuists, of the Busembaums and the Dianas, of the Liguoris and the Sanchezes, treating of transgressions against the sixth and ninth commandments of the Decalogue.

In awakening an almost divine ideal in this soul steeped in her precepts—a soul possibly predisposed to the teachings of the Church through hereditary influences dating back from the reign of Henry III, religion had also stirred the illegitimate, forbidden enjoyment of the senses. Licentious and mystical obsessions haunted his brain, they mingled confusedly, and he would often be troubled by an unappeasable desire to shun the vulgarities of the world and to plunge, far from the customs and modes held in such reverence, into convulsions and raptures which were holy or infernal and which, in either case, proved too exhausting and enervating.

He would arise prostrate from such reveries, fatigued and all but lifeless. He would light the lamps and candles so as to flood the room with light, for he hoped that by so doing he might possibly diminish the intolerably persistent and dull throbbing of his arteries which beat under his neck with redoubled strokes.

Chapter 10

During the course of this malady which attacks impoverished races, sudden calms succeed an attack. Strangely enough, Des Esseintes awoke one morning recovered; no longer was he tormented by the throbbing of his neck or by his racking cough. Instead, he had an ineffable sensation of contentment, a lightness of mind in which thought was sparklingly clear, turning from a turbid, opaque, green color to a liquid iridescence magical with tender rainbow tints.

This lasted several days. Then hallucinations of odor suddenly appeared.

His room was aromatic with the fragrance of frangipane; he tried to ascertain if a bottle were not uncorked—no! not a bottle was to be found in the room, and he passed into his study and thence to the kitchen. Still the odor persisted.

Des Esseintes rang for his servant and asked if he smelled anything. The domestic sniffed the air and declared he could not detect any perfume. There was no doubt about it: his nervous attacks had returned again, under the appearance of a new illusion of the senses.

Fatigued by the tenacity of this imaginary aroma, he resolved to steep himself in real perfumes, hoping that this homeopathic treatment would cure him or would at least drown the persistent odor.

He betook himself to his dressing room. There, near an old baptistery which he used as a wash basin, under a long mirror of forged iron, which, like the edge of a well silvered by the moon, confined the green dull surface of the mirror, were bottles of every conceivable size and form, placed on ivory shelves.

He set them on the table and divided them into two series: one of the simple perfumes, pure extracts or spirits, the other of compound perfumes, designated under the generic term of bouquets.

He sank into an easy chair and meditated.

He had long been skilled in the science of smell. He believed that this sense could give one delights equal to those of hearing and sight; each sense being susceptible, if naturally keen and if properly cultivated, to new impressions, which it could intensify, coordinate and compose into that unity which constitutes a creative work. And it was not more abnormal and unnatural that an art should be called into existence by disengaging odors than that another art should be evoked by detaching sound waves or by striking the eye with diversely colored rays. But if no person could discern, without intuition developed by study, a painting by a master from a daub, a melody of Beethoven from one by Clapisson, no more could any one at first, without preliminary initiation, help confusing a bouquet invented by a sincere artist with a pot pourri made by some manufacturer to be sold in groceries and bazaars.

In this art, the branch devoted to achieving certain effects by artificial methods particularly delighted him.

Perfumes, in fact, rarely come from the flowers whose names they bear. The artist who dared to borrow nature's elements would only produce a bastard work which would have neither authenticity nor style, inasmuch as the essence obtained by the distillation of flowers would bear but a distant and vulgar relation to the odor of the living flower, wafting its fragrance into the air.

Thus, with the exception of the inimitable jasmine which it is impossible to counterfeit, all flowers are perfectly represented by the blend of aromatic spirits, stealing the very personality of the model, and to it adding that nuance the more, that heady scent, that rare touch which entitled a thing to be called a work of art.

To resume, in the science of perfumery, the artist develops the natural odor of the flowers, working over his subject like a jeweler refining the lustre of a gem and making it precious.

Little by little, the arcana of this art, most neglected of all, was revealed to Des Esseintes who could now read this language, as diversified and insinuating as that of literature, this style with its unexpected concision under its vague flowing appearance.

To achieve this end he had first been compelled to master the grammar and understand the syntax of odors, learning the secret of the rules that regulate them, and, once familiarized with the dialect, he compared the works of the masters, of the Atkinsons and Lubins, the Chardins and Violets, the Legrands and Piesses; then he separated the construction of their phrases, weighed the value of their words and the arrangement of their periods.

Later on, in this idiom of fluids, experience was able to support theories too often incomplete and banal.

Classic perfumery, in fact, was scarcely diversified, almost colorless and uniformly issuing from the mold cast by the ancient chemists. It was in its dotage, confined to its old alambics, when the romantic period was born and had modified the old style, rejuvenating it, making it more supple and malleable.

Step by step, its history followed that of our language. The perfumed Louis XIII style, composed of elements highly prized at that time, of iris powder, musk, chive and myrtle water already designated under the name of "water of the angels," was hardly sufficient to express the cavalier graces, the rather crude tones of the period which certain sonnets of Saint-Amand have preserved for us. Later, with myrrh and olibanum, the mystic odors, austere and powerful, the pompous gesture of the great period, the redundant artifices of oratorial art, the full, sustained harmonious style of Bossuet and the masters of the pulpit were almost possible. Still later, the sophisticated, rather bored graces of French society under Louis XV, more easily found their interpretation in the almond which in a manner summed up this epoch; then, after the ennui and jadedness of the first empire, which misused Eau de Cologne and rosemary, perfumery rushed, in the wake of Victor Hugo and Gautier, towards the Levant. It created oriental combinations, vivid Eastern nosegays, discovered new intonations, antitheses which until then had been unattempted, selected and made use of antique nuances which it complicated, refined and assorted. It resolutely rejected that voluntary decrepitude to which it had been reduced by the Malesherbes, the Boileaus, the Andrieuxes and the Baour-Lormians, wretched distillers of their own poems.

But this language had not remained stationery since the period of 1830. It had continued to evolve and, patterning itself on the progress of the century, had advanced parallel with the other arts. It, too, had yielded to the desires of amateurs and artists, receiving its inspiration from the Chinese and Japanese, conceiving fragrant albums, imitating the Takeoka bouquets of flowers, obtaining the odor of Rondeletia from the blend of lavender and clove; the peculiar aroma of Chinese ink from the marriage of patchouli and camphor; the emanation of Japanese Hovenia by compounds of citron, clove and neroli.

Des Esseintes studied and analyzed the essences of these fluids, experimenting to corroborate their texts. He took pleasure in playing the rôle of a psychologist for his personal satisfaction, in taking apart and re-assembling the machinery of a work, in separating the pieces forming the structure of a compound exhalation, and his sense of smell had thereby attained a sureness that was all but perfect.

Just as a wine merchant has only to smell a drop of wine to recognize the grape, as a hop dealer determines the exact value of hops by sniffing a bag, as a Chinese trader can immediately tell the origin of the teas he smells, knowing in what farms of what mountains, in what Buddhistic convents it was cultivated, the very time when its leaves were gathered, the state and the degree of torrefaction, the effect upon it of its proximity to the plum-tree and other flowers, to all those perfumes which change its essence, adding to it an unexpected touch and introducing into its dryish flavor a hint of distant fresh flowers; just so could Des Esseintes, by inhaling a dash of perfume, instantly explain its mixture and the psychology of its blend, and could almost give the name of the artist who had composed and given it the personal mark of his individual style.

Naturally he had a collection of all the products used by perfumers. He even had the real Mecca balm, that rare balm cultivated only in certain parts of Arabia Petraea and under the monopoly of the ruler.

Now, seated in his dressing room in front of his table, he thought of creating a new bouquet; and he was overcome by that moment of wavering confidence familiar to writers when, after months of inaction, they prepare for a new work.

Like Balzac who was wont to scribble on many sheets of paper so as to put himself in a mood for work, Des Esseintes felt the necessity of steadying his hand by several initial and unimportant experiments. Desiring to create heliotrope, he took down bottles of vanilla and almond, then changed his idea and decided to experiment with sweet peas.

He groped for a long time, unable to effect the proper combinations, for orange is dominant in the fragrance of this flower. He attempted several combinations and ended in achieving the exact blend by joining tuberose and rose to orange, the whole united by a drop of vanilla.

His hesitation disappeared. He felt alert and ready for work; now he made some tea by blending cassie with iris, then, sure of his technique, he decided to proceed with a fulminating phrase whose thunderous roar would annihilate the insidious odor of almond still hovering over his room.

He worked with amber and with Tonkin musk, marvelously powerful; with patchouli, the most poignant of vegetable perfumes whose flower, in its habitat, wafts an odor of mildew. Try what he would, the eighteenth century obsessed him; the panier robes and furbelows appeared before his eyes; memories of Boucher's Venus haunted him; recollections of Themidor's romance, of the exquisite Rosette pursued him. Furious, he rose and to rid himself of the obsession, with all his strength he inhaled that pure essence of spikenard, so dear to Orientals and so repulsive to Europeans because of its pronounced odor of valerian. He was stunned by the violence of the shock. As though pounded by hammer strokes, the filigranes of the delicate odor disappeared; he profited by the period of respite to escape the dead centuries, the antiquated fumes, and to enter, as he formerly had done, less limited or more recent works.

He had of old loved to lull himself with perfumes. He used effects analogous to those of the poets, and employed the admirable order of certain pieces of Baudelaire, such as Irreparable and le Balcon, where the last of the five lines composing the strophe is the echo of the first verse and returns, like a refrain, to steep the soul in infinite depths of melancholy and languor.

He strayed into reveries evoked by those aromatic stanzas, suddenly brought to his point of departure, to the motive of his meditation, by the return of the initial theme, reappearing, at stated intervals, in the fragrant orchestration of the poem.

He actually wished to saunter through an astonishing, diversified landscape, and he began with a sonorous, ample phrase that suddenly opened a long vista of fields for him.

With his vaporizers, he injected an essence formed of ambrosia, lavender and sweet peas into this room; this formed an essence which, when distilled by an artist, deserves the name by which it is known: "extract of wild grass"; into this he introduced an exact blend of tuberose, orange flower and almond, and forthwith artificial lilacs sprang into being, while the linden-trees rustled, their thin emanations, imitated by extract of London tilia, drooping earthward.

Into this décor, arranged with a few broad lines, receding as far as the eye could reach, under his closed lids, he introduced a light rain of human and half feline essences, possessing the aroma of petticoats, breathing of the powdered, painted woman, the stephanotis, ayapana, opopanax, champaka, sarcanthus and cypress wine, to which he added a dash of syringa, in order to give to the artificial life of paints which they exhaled, a suggestion of natural dewy laughter and pleasures enjoyed in the open air.

Then, through a ventilator, he permitted these fragrant waves to escape, only preserving the field which he renewed, compelling it to return in his strophes like a ritornello.

The women had gradually disappeared. Now the plain had grown solitary. Suddenly, on the enchanted horizon, factories appeared whose tall chimneys flared like bowls of punch.

The odor of factories and of chemical products now passed with the breeze which was simulated by means of fans; nature exhaled its sweet effluvia amid this putrescence.

Des Esseintes warmed a pellet of storax, and a singular odor, at once repugnant and exquisite, pervaded the room. It partook of the delicious fragrance of jonquil and of the stench of gutta percha and coal oil. He disinfected his hands, inserted his resin in a hermetically sealed box, and the factories disappeared.

Then, among the revived vapors of the lindens and meadow grass, he threw several drops of new mown hay, and, amid this magic site for the moment despoiled of its lilacs, sheaves of hay were piled up, introducing a new season and scattering their fine effluence into these summer odors.

At last, when he had sufficiently enjoyed this sight, he suddenly scattered the exotic perfumes, emptied his vaporizers, threw in his concentrated spirits, poured his balms, and, in the exasperated and stifling heat of the room there rose a crazy sublimated nature, a paradoxical nature which was neither genuine nor charming, reuniting the tropical spices and the peppery breath of Chinese sandal wood and Jamaica hediosmia with the French odors of jasmine, hawthorn and verbena. Regardless of seasons and climates he forced trees of diverse essences into life, and flowers with conflicting fragrances and colors. By the clash of these tones he created a general, nondescript, unexpected, strange perfume in which reappeared, like an obstinate refrain, the decorative phrase of the beginning, the odor of the meadows fanned by the lilacs and lindens.

Suddenly a poignant pain seized him; he felt as though wimbles were drilling into his temples. Opening his eyes he found himself in his dressing room, seated in front of his table. Stupefied, he painfully walked across the room to the window which he half opened. A puff of wind dispelled the stifling atmosphere which was enveloping him. To exercise his limbs, he walked up and down gazing at the ceiling where crabs and sea-wrack stood out in relief against a background as light in color as the sands of the seashore. A similar décor covered the plinths and bordered the partitions which were covered with Japanese sea-green crêpe, slightly wrinkled, imitating a river rippled by the wind. In this light current swam a rose petal, around which circled a school of tiny fish painted with two strokes of the brush.

But his eyelids remained heavy. He ceased to pace about the short space between the baptistery and the bath; he leaned against the window. His dizziness ended. He carefully stopped up the vials, and used the occasion to arrange his cosmetics. Since his arrival at Fontenay he had not touched them; and now was quite astonished to behold once more this collection formerly visited by so many women. The flasks and jars were lying heaped up against each other. Here, a porcelain box contained a marvelous white cream which, when applied on the cheeks, turns to a tender rose color, under the action of the air—to such a true flesh-color that it procures the very illusion of a skin touched with blood; there, lacquer objects incrusted with mother of pearl enclosed Japanese gold and Athenian green, the color of the cantharis wing, gold and green which change to deep purple when wetted; there were jars filled with filbert paste, the serkis of the harem, emulsions of lilies, lotions of strawberry water and elders for the complexion, and tiny bottles filled with solutions of Chinese ink and rose water for the eyes. There were tweezers, scissors, rouge and powder-puffs, files and beauty patches.

He handled this collection, formerly bought to please a mistress who swooned under the influence of certain aromatics and balms,—a nervous, unbalanced woman who loved to steep the nipples of her breasts in perfumes, but who never really experienced a delicious and overwhelming ecstacy save when her head was scraped with a comb or when she could inhale, amid caresses, the odor of perspiration, or the plaster of unfinished houses on rainy days, or of dust splashed by huge drops of rain during summer storms.

He mused over these memories, and one afternoon spent at Pantin through idleness and curiosity, in company with this woman at the home of one of her sisters, returned to him, stirring in him a forgotten world of old ideas and perfumes; while the two women prattled and displayed their gowns, he had drawn near the window and had seen, through the dusty panes, the muddy street sprawling before him, and had heard the repeated sounds of galoches over the puddles of the pavement.

This scene, already far removed, came to him suddenly, strangely and vividly. Pantin was there before him, animated and throbbing in this greenish and dull mirror into which his unseeing eyes plunged. A hallucination transported him far from Fontenay. Beside reflecting the street, the mirror brought back thoughts it had once been instrumental in evoking, and plunged in revery, he repeated to himself this ingenious, sad and comforting composition he had formerly written upon returning to Paris:

"Yes, the season of downpours is come. Now behold water-spouts vomiting as they rush over the pavements, and rubbish marinates in puddles that fill the holes scooped out of the macadam.

"Under a lowering sky, in the damp air, the walls of houses have black perspiration and their air-holes are fetid; the loathsomeness of existence increases and melancholy overwhelms one; the seeds of vileness which each person harbors in his soul, sprout. The craving for vile debaucheries seizes austere people and base desires grow rampant in the brains of respectable men.

"And yet I warm myself, here before a cheerful fire. From a basket of blossoming flowers comes the aroma of balsamic benzoin, geranium and the whorl-flowered bent-grass which permeates the room. In the very month of November, at Pantin, in the rue de Paris, springtime persists. Here in my solitude I laugh at the fears of families which, to shun the approaching cold weather, escape on every steamer to Cannes and to other winter resorts.

"Inclement nature does nothing to contribute to this extraordinary phenomenon. It must be said that his artificial season at Pantin is the result of man's ingenuity.

"In fact, these flowers are made of taffeta and are mounted on wire. The springtime odor filters through the window joints, exhaled from the neighboring factories, from the perfumeries of Pinaud and Saint James.

"For the workmen exhausted by the hard labors of the plants, for the young employes who too often are fathers, the illusion of a little healthy air is possible, thanks to these manufacturers.

"So, from this fabulous subterfuge of a country can an intelligent cure arise. The consumptive men about town who are sent to the South die, their end due to the change in their habits and to the nostalgia for the Parisian excesses which destroyed them. Here, under an artificial climate, libertine memories will reappear, the languishing feminine emanations evaporated by the factories. Instead of the deadly ennui of provincial life, the doctor can thus platonically substitute for his patient the atmosphere of the Parisian women and of boudoirs. Most often, all that is necessary to effect the cure is for the subject to have a somewhat fertile imagination.

"Since, nowadays, nothing genuine exists, since the wine one drinks and the liberty one boldly proclaims are laughable and a sham, since it really needs a healthy dose of good will to believe that the governing classes are respectable and that the lower classes are worthy of being assisted or pitied, it seems to me," concluded Des Esseintes, "to be neither ridiculous nor senseless, to ask of my fellow men a quantity of illusion barely equivalent to what they spend daily in idiotic ends, so as to be able to convince themselves that the town of Pantin is an artificial Nice or a Menton.

"But all this does not prevent me from seeing," he said, forced by weakness from his meditations, "that I must be careful to mistrust these delicious and abominable practices which may ruin my constitution." He sighed. "Well, well, more pleasures to moderate, more precautions to be taken."

And he passed into his study, hoping the more easily to escape the spell of these perfumes.

He opened the window wide, glad to be able to breath the air. But it suddenly seemed to him that the breeze brought in a vague tide of bergamot with which jasmine and rose water were blent. Agitated, he asked himself whether he was not really under the yoke of one of those possessions exercised in the Middle Ages. The odor changed and was transformed, but it persisted. A faint scent of tincture of tolu, of balm of Peru and of saffron, united by several drams of amber and musk, now issued from the sleeping village and suddenly, the metamorphosis was effected, those scattered elements were blent, and once more the frangipane spread from the valley of Fontenay as far as the fort, assailing his exhausted nostrils, once more shattering his helpless nerves and throwing him into such a prostration that he fell unconscious on the window sill.

Chapter 11

The servants were seized with alarm and lost no time in calling the Fontenay physician who was completely at sea about Des Esseintes' condition. He mumbled a few medical terms, felt his pulse, examined the invalid's tongue, unsuccessfully sought to make him speak, prescribed sedatives and rest, promised to return on the morrow and, at the negative sign made by Des Esseintes who recovered enough strength to chide the zeal of his servants and to bid farewell to this intruder, he departed and was soon retailing through the village the eccentricities of this house whose decorations had positively amazed him and held him rooted to the spot.

To the great astonishment of the domestics, who no longer dared stir from the servants' quarters, their master recovered in a few days, and they surprised him drumming against the window panes, gazing at the sky with a troubled look.

One afternoon the bells were peremptorily rung and Des Esseintes commanded his trunks to be packed for a long voyage.

While the man and the woman were choosing, under his guidance, the necessary equipment, he feverishly paced up and down the cabin of the dining room, consulted the timetables of the steamers, walked through his study where he continued to gaze at the clouds with an air at once impatient and satisfied.

For a whole week, the weather had been atrocious. Streams of soot raced unceasing across the grey fields of the sky-masses of clouds like rocks torn from the earth.

At intervals, showers swept downward, engulfing the valley with torrents of rain.

Today, the appearance of the heavens had changed. The rivers of ink had evaporated and vanished, and the harsh contours of the clouds had softened. The sky was uniformly flat and covered with a brackish film.

Little by little, this film seemed to drop, and a watery haze covered the country side. The rain no longer fell in cataracts as on the preceding evening; instead, it fell incessantly, fine, sharp and penetrating; it inundated the walks, covered the roads with its innumerable threads which joined heaven and earth. The livid sky threw a wan leaden light on the village which was now transformed into a lake of mud pricked by needles of water that dotted the puddles with drops of bright silver. In this desolation of nature, everything was gray, and only the housetops gleamed against the dead tones of the walls.

"What weather!" sighed the aged domestic, placing on a chair the clothes which his master had requested of him—an outfit formerly ordered from London.

Des Esseintes' sole response was to rub his hands and to sit down in front of a book-case with glass doors. He examined the socks which had been placed nearby for his inspection. For a moment he hesitated on the color; then he quickly studied the melancholy day and earnestly bethought himself of the effect he desired. He chose a pair the color of feuillemort, quickly slipped them on, put on a pair of buttoned shoes, donned the mouse grey suit which was checquered with a lava gray and dotted with black, placed a small hunting cap on his head and threw a blue raincoat over him. He reached the railway station, followed by the servant who almost bent under the weight of a trunk, a valise, a carpet bag, a hat box and a traveling rug containing umbrellas and canes. He informed his servant that the date of his return was problematical, that he might return in a year, in a month, in a week, or even sooner, and enjoined him to change nothing in the house. He gave a sum of money which he thought would be necessary for the upkeep of the house during his absence, and climbed into the coach, leaving the old man astounded, arms waving and mouth gaping, behind the rail, while the train got under way.

He was alone in his compartment; a vague and dirty country side, such as one sees through an aquarium of troubled water, receded rapidly behind the train which was lashed by the rain. Plunged in his meditations, Des Esseintes closed his eyes.

Once more, this so ardently desired and finally attained solitude had ended in a fearful distress. This silence which formerly would have appeared as a compensation for the stupidities heard for years, now weighed on him with an unendurable burden. One morning he had awakened, as uneasy as a prisoner in his cell; his lips had sought to articulate sounds, tears had welled to his eyes and he had found it impossible to breathe, suffocating like a person who had sobbed for hours.

Seized with a desire to walk, to behold a human figure, to speak to someone, to mingle with life, he had proceeded to call his domestics, employing a specious pretext; but conversation with them was impossible. Besides the fact that these old people, bowed down by years of silence and the customs of attendants, were almost dumb, the distance at which Des Esseintes had always kept them was hardly conducive to inducing them to open their mouths now. Too, they possessed dull brains and were incapable of answering his questions other than by monosyllables.

It was impossible, therefore, to find any solace in their society; but a new phenomenon now occurred. The reading of the novels of Dickens, which he had lately undertaken to soothe his nerves and which had only produced effects the opposite of those hoped for, began slowly to act in an unexpected manner, bringing on visions of English existence on which he mused for hours; little by little, in these fictive contemplations, ideas insinuated themselves, ideas of the voyage brought to an end, of verified dreams on which was imposed the desire to experience new impressions, and thus escape the exhausting cerebral debauches intent upon beating in the void.

With its mist and rain, this abominable weather aided his thoughts still more, by reinforcing the memories of his readings, by placing under his eyes the unfading image of a land of fog and mud, and by refusing to let his ideas wander idly.

One day, able to endure it no longer, he had instantly decided. Such was his haste that he even took flight before the designated time, for he wished to shun the present moment, wished to find himself jostled and shouldered in the hubbub of crowded streets and railway stations.

"I breathe!" he exclaimed when the train moderated its waltz and stopped in the Sceaux station rotunda, panting while its wheels performed its last pirouettes.

Once in the boulevard d'Enfer, he hailed a coachman. In some strange manner he extracted a pleasure from the fact that he was so hampered with trunks and rugs. By promising a substantial tip, he reached an understanding with the man of the brown trousers and red waistcoat.

"At once!" he commanded. "And when you reach the rue de Rivoli, stop in front of Galignani's Messenger." Before departing, he desired to buy a Baedeker or Murray guide of London.

The carriage got under way heavily, raising rings of mud around its wheels and moving through marsh-like ground. Beneath the gray sky which seemed suspended over the house tops, water gushed down the thick sides of the high walls, spouts overflowed, and the streets were coated with a slimy dirt in which passersby slipped. Thickset men paused on sidewalks bespattered by passing omnibuses, and women, their skirts tucked up to the knees, bent under umbrellas, flattened themselves against the shops to avoid being splashed.

The rain entered diagonally through the carriage doors. Des Esseintes was obliged to lift the carriage windows down which the water ran, while drops of mud furrowed their way like fireworks on each side of the fiacre. To the monotonous sound of sacks of peas shaking against his head through the action of the showers pattering against the trunks and on the carriage rug, Des Esseintes dreamed of his voyage. This already was a partial realization of his England, enjoyed in Paris through the means of this frightful weather: a rainy, colossal London smelling of molten metal and of soot, ceaselessly steaming and smoking in the fog now spread out before his eyes; then rows of docks sprawled ahead, as far as the eye could reach, docks full of cranes, hand winches and bales, swarming with men perched on masts or astride yard sails, while myriads of other men on the quays pushed hogsheads into cellars.

All this was transpiring in vast warehouses along the river banks which were bathed by the muddy and dull water of an imaginary Thames, in a forest of masts and girders piercing the wan clouds of the firmament, while trains rushed past at full speed or rumpled underground uttering horrible cries and vomiting waves of smoke, and while, through every street, monstrous and gaudy and infamous advertisements flared through the eternal twilight, and strings of carriages passed between rows of preoccupied and taciturn people whose eyes stared ahead and whose elbows pressed closely against their bodies.

Des Esseintes shivered deliciously to feel himself mingling in this terrible world of merchants, in this insulating mist, in this incessant activity, in this pitiless gearing which ground millions of the disinherited, urged by the comfort-distilling philanthropists to recite Biblical verses and to sing psalms.

Then the vision faded suddenly with a jolt of the fiacre which made him rebound in his seat. He gazed through the carriage windows. Night had fallen; gas burners blinked through the fog, amid a yellowish halo; ribbons of fire swam in puddles of water and seemed to revolve around wheels of carriages moving through liquid and dirty flame. He endeavored to get his bearings, perceived the Carrousel and suddenly, unreasoningly, perhaps through the simple effect of the high fall from fanciful spaces, his thought reverted to a very trivial incident. He remembered that his domestic had neglected to put a tooth brush in his belongings. Then, he passed in review the list of objects packed up; everything had been placed in his valise, but the annoyance of having omitted this brush persisted until the driver, pulling up, broke the chain of his reminiscences and regrets.

He was in the rue de Rivoli, in front of Galignani's Messenger. Separated by a door whose unpolished glass was covered with inscriptions and with strips of passe-partout framing newspaper clippings and telegrams, were two vast shop windows crammed with albums and books. He drew near, attracted by the sight of these books bound in parrot-blue and cabbage-green paper, embossed with silver and golden letterings. All this had an anti-Parisian touch, a mercantile appearance, more brutal and yet less wretched than those worthless bindings of French books; here and there, in the midst of the opened albums, reproducing humorous scenes from Du Maurier and John Leech, or the delirious cavalcades of Caldecott, some French novels appeared, blending placid and satisfied vulgarities to these rich verjuice hues. He tore himself away from his contemplation, opened the door and entered a large library which was full of people. Seated strangers unfolded maps and jabbered in strange languages. A clerk brought him a complete collection of guides. He, in turns, sat down to examine the books with their flexible covers. He glanced through them and paused at a page of the Baedeker describing the London museums. He became interested in the laconic and exact details of the guide books, but his attention wandered away from the old English paintings to the moderns which attracted him much more. He recalled certain works he had seen at international expositions, and imagined that he might possibly behold them once more at London: pictures by Millais—the Eve of Saint Agnes with its lunar clear green; pictures by Watts, strange in color, checquered with gamboge and indigo, pictures sketched by a sick Gustave Moreau, painted by an anæmic Michael Angelo and retouched by a Raphael submerged in blue. Among other canvasses, he recalled a Denunciation of Cain, an Ida, some Eves where, in the strange and mysterious mixture of these three masters, rose the personality, at once refined and crude, of a learned and dreamy Englishman tormented by the bewitchment of cruel tones.

These canvasses thronged through his memory. The clerk, astonished by this client who was so lost to the world, asked him which of the guides he would take. Des Esseintes remained dumbfounded, then excused himself, bought a Baedeker and departed. The dampness froze him to the spot; the wind blew from the side, lashing the arcades with whips of rain. "Proceed to that place," he said to the driver, pointing with his finger to the end of a passage where a store formed the angle of the rue de Rivoli and the rue Castiglione and, with its whitish panes of glass illumed from within, resembled a vast night lamp burning through the wretchedness of this mist, in the misery of this crazy weather.

It was the Bodega. Des Esseintes strayed into a large room sustained by iron pillars and lined, on each side of its walls, with tall barrels placed on their ends upon gantries, hooped with iron, their paunches with wooden loopholes imitating a rack of pipes and from whose notches hung tulip-shaped glasses, upside down. The lower sides were bored and hafted with stone cocks. These hogsheads painted with a royal coat of arms displayed the names of their drinks, the contents, and the prices on colored labels and stated that they were to be purchased by the cask, by the bottle or by the glass.

In the passage between these rows of casks, under the gas jets which flared at one end of an ugly iron-gray chandelier, tables covered with baskets of Palmers biscuits, hard and salty cakes, plates piled with mince pies and sandwiches concealing strong, mustardy concoctions under their unsavory covers, succeeded each other between a row of seats and as far as the end of this cellar which was lined with still more hogsheads carrying tiny barrels on their tops, resting on their sides and bearing their names stamped with hot metal into the oak.

An odor of alcohol assailed Des Esseintes upon taking a seat in this room heavy with strong wines. He looked about him. Here, the tuns were placed in a straight line, exhibiting the whole series of ports, the sweet or sour wines the color of mahogany or amaranth, and distinguished by such laudatory epithets as old port, light delicate, Cockburn's very fine, magnificent old Regina. There, protruding formidable abdomens pressed closely against each other, huge casks contained the martial Spanish wines, sherry and its derivatives, the san lucar, pasto, pale dry, oloroso and amontilla.

The cellar was filled with people. Leaning on his elbows on a corner of the table, Des Esseintes sat waiting for his glass of port ordered of a gentleman who was opening explosive sodas contained in oval bottles which recalled, while exaggerating, the capsules of gelatine and gluten used by pharmacies to conceal the taste of certain medicines.

Englishmen were everywhere,—awkward pale clergymen garbed in black from head to foot, with soft hats, laced shoes, very long coats dotted in the front with tiny buttons, clean-shaved chins, round spectacles, greasy flat hair; faces of tripe dealers and mastiff snouts with apoplectic necks, ears like tomatoes, vinous cheeks, blood-shot crazy eyes, whiskers that looked like those of some big monkeys; farther away, at the end of the wine store, a long row of tow-headed individuals, their chins covered with white hair like the end of an artichoke, reading, through a microscope, the tiny roman type of an English newspaper; opposite him, a sort of American commodore, dumpy and thick-set, with smoked skin and bulbous nose, was sleeping, a cigar planted in the hairy aperture of his mouth. Opposite were frames hanging on the wall enclosing advertisements of Champagne, the trade marks of Perrier and

Roederer, Heidsieck and Mumm, and a hooded head of a monk, with the name of Dom Perignon, Rheims, written in Gothic characters.

A certain enervation enveloped Des Esseintes in this guard house atmosphere; stunned by the prattle of the Englishmen conversing among themselves, he fell into a revery, evoking, before the purple port which filled the glasses, the creatures of Dickens that love this drink so very much, imaginatively peopling the cellar with new personages, seeing here, the white head of hair and the ruddy complexion of Mr. Wickfield; there, the phlegmatic, crafty face and the vengeful eye of Mr. Tulkinghorn, the melancholy solicitor in Bleak House. Positively, all of them broke away from his memory and installed themselves in the Bodega, with their peculiar characteristics and their betraying gestures. His memories, brought to life by his recent readings, attained a startling precision. The city of the romancer, the house illumined and warmed, so perfectly tended and isolated, the bottles poured slowly by little Dorrit and Dora Copperfield and Tom Pinch's sister, appeared to him sailing like an ark in a deluge of mire and soot. Idly he wandered through this imaginary London, happy to be sheltered, as he listened to the sinister shrieks of tugs plying up and down the Thames. His glass was empty. Despite the heavy fumes in this cellar, caused by the cigars and pipes, he experienced a cold shiver when he returned to the reality of the damp and fetid weather.

He called for a glass of amontillado, and suddenly, beside this pale, dry wine, the lenitive, sweetish stories of the English author were routed, to be replaced by the pitiless revulsives and the grievous irritants of Edgar Allen Poe; the cold nightmares of The Cask of Amontillado, of the man immured in a vault, assailed him; the ordinary placid faces of American and English drinkers who occupied the room, appeared to him to reflect involuntary frightful thoughts, to be harboring instinctive, odious plots. Then he perceived that he was left alone here and that the dinner hour was near. He payed his bill, tore himself from his seat and dizzily gained the door. He received a wet slap in the face upon leaving the place. The street lamps moved their tiny fans of flame which failed to illuminate; the sky had dropped to the very houses. Des Esseintes viewed the arcades of the rue de Rivoli, drowned in the gloom and submerged by water, and it seemed to him that he was in the gloomy tunnel under the Thames. Twitchings of his stomach recalled him to reality. He regained his carriage, gave the driver the address of the tavern in the rue d'Amsterdam near the station, and looked at his watch: seven o'clock. He had just time to eat dinner; the train would not leave until ten minutes of nine, and he counted on his fingers, reckoning the hours of travel from Dieppe to Newhaven, saying to himself: "If the figures of the timetable are correct, I shall be at London tomorrow at twelve-thirty."

The fiacre stopped in front of the tavern. Once more, Des Esseintes alighted and entered a long dark plain room, divided into partitions as high as a man's waist,—a series of compartments resembling stalls. In this room, wider towards the door, many beer pumps stood on a counter, near hams having the color of old violins, red lobsters, marinated mackerel, with onions and carrots, slices of lemon, bunches of laurel and thym, juniper berries and long peppers swimming in thick sauce.

One of these boxes was unoccupied. He took it and called a young black-suited man who bent forward, muttering something in a jargon he could not understand. While the cloth was being laid, Des Esseintes viewed his neighbors. They were islanders, just as at the Bodega, with cold faience eyes, crimson complexions, thoughtful or haughty airs. They were reading foreign newspapers. The only ones eating were unescorted women in pairs, robust English women with boyish faces, large teeth, ruddy apple cheeks, long hands and legs. They attacked, with genuine ardor, a rumpsteak pie, a warm meat dish cooked in mushroom sauce and covered with a crust, like a pie.

After having lacked appetite for such a long time, he remained amazed in the presence of these hearty eaters whose voracity whetted his hunger. He ordered oxtail soup and enjoyed it heartily. Then he glanced at the menu for the fish, ordered a haddock and, seized with a sudden pang of hunger at the sight of so many people relishing their food, he ate some roast beef and drank two pints of ale, stimulated by the flavor of a cow-shed which this fine, pale beer exhaled.

His hunger persisted. He lingered over a piece of blue Stilton cheese, made quick work of a rhubarb tart, and to vary his drinking, quenched his thirst with porter, that dark beer which smells of Spanish licorice but which does not have its sugary taste.

He breathed deeply. Not for years had he eaten and drunk so much. This change of habit, this choice of unexpected and solid food had awakened his stomach from its long sleep. He leaned back in his chair, lit a cigarette and prepared to sip his coffee into which gin had been poured.

The rain continued to fall. He heard it patter on the panes which formed a ceiling at the end of the room; it fell in cascades down the spouts. No one was stirring in the room. Everybody, utterly weary, was indulging himself in front of his wine glass.

Tongues were now wagging freely. As almost all the English men and women raised their eyes as they spoke, Des Esseintes concluded that they were talking of the bad weather; not one of them laughed. He threw a delighted glance on their suits whose color and cut did not perceivably differ from that of others, and he experienced a sense of contentment in not being out of tune in this environment, of being, in some way, though superficially, a naturalized London citizen. Then he suddenly started. "And what about the train?" he asked himself. He glanced at his watch: ten minutes to eight. "I still have nearly a half-hour to remain here." Once more, he began to muse upon the plan he had conceived.

In his sedentary life, only two countries had ever attracted him: Holland and England.

He had satisfied the first of his desires. Unable to keep away, one fine day he had left Paris and visited the towns of the Low Lands, one by one.

In short, nothing but cruel disillusions had resulted from this trip. He had fancied a Holland after the works of Teniers and Steen, of Rembrandt and Ostade, in his usual way imagining rich, unique and incomparable Ghettos, had thought of amazing kermesses, continual debauches in the country sides, intent for a view of that patriarchal simplicity, that jovial lusty spirit celebrated by the old masters.

Certainly, Haarlem and Amsterdam had enraptured him. The unwashed people, seen in their country farms, really resembled those types painted by Van Ostade, with their uncouth children and their old fat women, embossed with huge breasts and enormous bellies. But of the unrestrained joys, the drunken family carousals, not a whit. He had to admit that the Dutch paintings at the Louvre had misled him. They had simply served as a springing board for his dreams. He had rushed forward on a false track and had wandered into capricious visions, unable to discover in the land itself, anything of that real and magical country which he had hoped to behold, seeing nothing at all, on the plots of ground strewn with barrels, of the dances of petticoated and stockinged peasants crying for very joy, stamping their feet out of sheer happiness and laughing loudly.

Decidedly nothing of all this was visible. Holland was a country just like any other country, and what was more, a country in no wise primitive, not at all simple, for the Protestant religion with its formal hypocricies and solemn rigidness held sway here.

The memory of that disenchantment returned to him. Once more he glanced at his watch: ten minutes still separated him from the train's departure. "It is about time to ask for the bill and leave," he told himself.

He felt an extreme heaviness in his stomach and through his body. "Come!" he addressed himself, "let us drink and screw up our courage." He filled a glass of brandy, while asking for the reckoning. An individual in black suit and with a napkin under one arm, a sort of majordomo with a bald and sharp head, a greying beard without moustaches, came forward. A pencil rested behind his ear and he assumed an attitude like a singer, one foot in front of the other; he drew a note book from his pocket, and without glancing at his paper, his eyes fixed on the ceiling, near a chandelier, wrote while counting. "There you are!" he said, tearing the sheet from his note book and giving it to Des Esseintes who looked at him with curiosity, as though he were a rare animal. What a surprising John Bull, he thought, contemplating this phlegmatic person who had, because of his shaved mouth, the appearance of a wheelsman of an American ship.

At this moment, the tavern door opened. Several persons entered bringing with them an odor of wet dog to which was blent the smell of coal wafted by the wind through the opened door. Des Esseintes was incapable of moving a limb. A soft warm languor prevented him from even stretching out his hand to light a cigar. He told himself: "Come now, let us get up, we must take ourselves off." Immediate objections thwarted his orders. What is the use of moving, when one can travel on a chair so magnificently? Was he not even now in London, whose aromas and atmosphere and inhabitants, whose food and utensils surrounded him? For what could he hope, if not new disillusionments, as had happened to him in Holland?

He had but sufficient time to race to the station. An overwhelming aversion for the trip, an imperious need of remaining tranquil, seized him with a more and more obvious and stubborn strength. Pensively, he let the minutes pass, thus cutting off all retreat, and he said to himself, "Now it would be necessary to rush to the gate and crowd into the baggage room! What ennui! What a bore that would be!" Then he repeated to himself once more, "In fine, I have experienced and seen all I wished to experience and see. I have been filled with English life since my departure. I would be mad indeed to go and, by an awkward trip, lose those imperishable sensations. How stupid of me to have sought to disown my old ideas, to have doubted the efficacy of the docile phantasmagories of my brain, like a very fool to have thought of the necessity, of the curiosity, of the interest of an excursion!"

"Well!" he exclaimed, consulting his watch, "it is now time to return home."

This time, he arose and left, ordered the driver to bring him back to the Sceaux station, and returned with his trunks, packages, valises, rugs, umbrellas and canes, to Fontenay, feeling the physical stimulation and the moral fatigue of a man coming back to his home after a long and dangerous voyage.

Chapter 12

During the days following his return, Des Esseintes contemplated his books and experienced, at the thought that he might have been separated from them for a long period, a satisfaction as complete as that which comes after a protracted absence. Under the touch of this sentiment, these objects possessed a renewed novelty to his mind, and he perceived in them beauties forgotten since the time he had purchased them.

Everything there, books, bric-a-brac and furniture, had an individual charm for him. His bed seemed the softer by comparison with the hard bed he would have occupied in London. The silent, discreet ministrations of his servants charmed him, exhausted as he was at the thought of the loud loquacity of hotel attendants. The methodical organization of his life made him feel that it was especially to be envied since the possibility of traveling had become imminent.

He steeped himself in this bath of habitude, to which artificial regrets insinuated a tonic quality.

But his books chiefly preoccupied him. He examined them, re-arranged them on the shelves, anxious to learn if the hot weather and the rains had damaged the bindings and injured the rare paper.

He began by moving all his Latin books; then he arranged in a new order the special works of Archelaus, Albert le Grand, Lully and Arnaud de Villanova treating of cabbala and the occult sciences; finally he examined his modern books, one by one, and was happy to perceive that all had remained intact.

This collection had cost him a considerable sum of money. He would not suffer, in his library, the books he loved to resemble other similar volumes, printed on cotton paper with the watermarks of Auvergne.

Formerly in Paris he had ordered made, for himself alone, certain volumes which specially engaged mechanics printed from hand presses.

Sometimes, he applied to Perrin of Lyons, whose graceful, clear type was suitable for archaic reprints of old books. At other times he dispatched orders to England or to America for the execution of modern literature and the works of the present century. Still again, he applied to a house in Lille, which for centuries had possessed a complete set of Gothic characters; he also would send requisitions to the old Enschede printing house of Haarlem whose foundry still has the stamps and dies of certain antique letters.

He had followed the same method in selecting his papers. Finally growing weary of the snowy Chinese and the nacreous and gilded Japanese papers, the white Whatmans, the brown Hollands, the buff-colored Turkeys and Seychal Mills, and equally disgusted with all mechanically manufactured sheets, he had ordered special laid paper in the mould, from the old plants of Vire which still employ the pestles once in use to grind hemp. To introduce a certain variety into his collection, he had repeatedly brought from London prepared stuffs, paper interwoven with hairs, and as a mark of his disdain for bibliophiles, he had a Lubeck merchant prepare for him an improved candle paper of bottle-blue tint, clear and somewhat brittle, in the pulp of which the straw was replaced by golden spangles resembling those which dot Danzig brandy.

Under these circumstances he had succeeded in procuring unique books, adopting obsolete formats which he had bound by Lortic, by Trautz-Bauzonnet or Chambolle, by the successors of Capé, in irreproachable covers of old silk, stamped cow hide, Cape goat skin, in full bindings with compartments and in mosaic designs, protected by tabby or moire watered silk, ecclesiastically ornamented with clasps and corners, and sometimes even enamelled by Gruel Engelmann with silver oxide and clear enamels.

Thus, with the marvelous episcopal lettering used in the old house of Le Clere, he had Baudelaire's works printed in a large format recalling that of ancient missals, on a very light and spongy Japan paper, soft as elder pith and imperceptibly tinted with a light rose hue through its milky white. This edition, limited to one copy, printed with a velvety black Chinese ink, had been covered outside and then recovered within with a wonderful genuine sow skin, chosen among a thousand, the color of flesh, its surface spotted where the hairs had been and adorned with black silk stamped in cold iron in miraculous designs by a great artist.

That day, Des Esseintes took this incomparable book from his shelves and handled it devotedly, once more reading certain pieces which seemed to him, in this simple but inestimable frame, more than ordinarily penetrating.

His admiration for this writer was unqualified. According to him, until Baudelaire's advent in literature, writers had limited themselves to exploring the surfaces of the soul or to penetrating into the accessible and illuminated caverns, restoring here and there the layers of capital sins, studying their veins, their growths, and noting, like Balzac for example, the layers of strata in the soul possessed by the monomania of a passion, by ambition, by avarice, by paternal stupidity, or by senile love.

What had been treated heretofore was the abundant health of virtues and of vices, the tranquil functioning of commonplace brains, and the practical reality of contemporary ideas, without any ideal of sickly depravation or of any beyond. In short, the discoveries of those analysts had stopped at the speculations of good or evil classified by the Church. It was the simple investigation, the conventional examination of a botanist minutely observing the anticipated development of normal efflorescence abounding in the natural earth.

Baudelaire had gone farther. He had descended to the very bowels of the inexhaustible mine, had involved his mind in abandoned and unfamiliar levels, and come to those districts of the soul where monstrous vegetations of thought extend their branches.

There, near those confines, the haunt of aberrations and of sickness, of the mystic lockjaw, the warm fever of lust, and the typhoids and vomits of crime, he had found, brooding under the gloomy clock of Ennui, the terrifying spectre of the age of sentiments and ideas.

He had revealed the morbid psychology of the mind which has attained the October of its sensations, recounted the symptoms of souls summoned by grief and licensed by spleen, and shown the increasing decay of impressions while the enthusiasms and beliefs of youth are enfeebled and the only thing remaining is the arid memory of miseries borne, intolerances endured and affronts suffered by intelligences oppressed by a ridiculous destiny.

He had pursued all the phases of that lamentable autumn, studying the human creature, quick to exasperation, ingenious in deceiving himself, compelling his thoughts to cheat each other so as to suffer the more keenly, and frustrating in advance all possible joy by his faculty of analysis and observation.

Then, in this vexed sensibility of the soul, in this ferocity of reflection that repels the restless ardor of devotions and the well-meaning outrages of charity, he gradually saw arising the horror of those senile passions, those ripe loves, where one person yields while the other is still suspicious, where lassitude denies such couples the filial caresses whose apparent youthfulness seems new, and the maternal candors whose gentleness and comfort impart, in a sense, the engaging remorse of a vague incest.

In magnificent pages he exposed his hybrid loves who were exasperated by the impotence in which they were overwhelmed, the hazardous deceits of narcotics and poisons invoked to aid in calming suffering and conquering ennui. At an epoch when literature attributed unhappiness of life almost exclusively to the mischances of unrequited love or to the jealousies that attend adulterous love, he disregarded such puerile maladies and probed into those wounds which are more fatal, more keen and deep, which arise from satiety, disillusion and scorn in ruined souls whom the present tortures, the past fills with loathing and the future frightens and menaces with despair.

And the more Des Esseintes read Baudelaire, the more he felt the ineffable charm of this writer who, in an age when verse served only to portray the external semblance of beings and things, had succeeded in expressing the inexpressible in a muscular and brawny language; who, more than any other writer possessed a marvelous power to define with a strange robustness of expression, the most fugitive and tentative morbidities of exhausted minds and sad souls.

After Baudelaire's works, the number of French books given place in his shelves was strictly limited. He was completely indifferent to those works which it is fashionable to praise. "The broad laugh of Rabelais," and "the deep comedy of Moliere," did not succeed in diverting him, and the antipathy he felt against these farces was so great that he did not hesitate to liken them, in the point of art, to the capers of circus clowns.

As for old poetry, he read hardly anything except Villon, whose melancholy ballads touched him, and, here and there, certain fragments from d'Aubigné, which stimulated his blood with the incredible vehemence of their apostrophes and curses.

In prose, he cared little for Voltaire and Rousseau, and was unmoved even by Diderot, whose so greatly praised Salons he found strangely saturated with moralizing twaddle and futility; in his hatred toward all this balderdash, he limited himself almost exclusively to the reading of Christian eloquence, to the books of Bourdaloue and Bossuet whose sonorously embellished periods were imposing; but, still more, he relished suggestive ideas condensed into severe and strong phrases, such as those created by Nicole in his reflections, and especially Pascal, whose austere pessimism and attrition deeply touched him.

Apart from such books as these, French literature began in his library with the nineteenth century.

This section was divided into two groups, one of which included the ordinary, secular literature, and the other the Catholic literature, a special but little known literature published by large publishing houses and circulated to the four corners of the earth.

He had had the hardihood to explore such crypts as these, just as in the secular art he had discovered, under an enormous mass of insipid writings, a few books written by true masters.

The distinctive character of this literature was the constant immutability of its ideas and language. Just as the Church perpetuated the primitive form of holy objects, so she has preserved the relics of her dogmas, piously retaining, as the frame that encloses them, the oratorical language of the celebrated century. As one of the Church's own writers, Ozanam, has put it, the Christian style needed only to make use of the dialect employed by Bourdaloue and by Bossuet to the exclusion of all else.

In spite of this statement, the Church, more indulgent, closed its eyes to certain expressions, certain turns of style borrowed from the secular language of the same century, and the Catholic idiom had slightly purified itself of its heavy and massive phrases, especially cleaning itself, in Bossuet, of its prolixity and the painful rallying of its pronouns; but here ended the concessions, and others would doubtless have been purposeless for the prose sufficed without this ballast for the limited range of subjects to which the Church confined itself.

Incapable of grappling with contemporary life, of rendering the most simple aspects of things and persons visible and palpable, unqualified to explain the complicated wiles of intellects indifferent to the benefits of salvation, this language was nevertheless excellent when it treated of abstract subjects. It proved valuable in the argument of controversy, in the demonstration of a theory, in the obscurity of a commentary and, more than any other style, had the necessary authority to affirm, without any discussion, the intent of a doctrine.

Unfortunately, here as everywhere, the sanctuary had been invaded by a numerous army of pedants who smirched by their ignorance and lack of talent the Church's noble and austere attire. Further to profane it, devout women had interfered, and stupid sacristans and foolish salons had acclaimed as works of genius the wretched prattle of such women.

Among such works, Des Esseintes had had the curiosity to read those of Madame Swetchine, the Russian, whose house in Paris was the rendezvous of the most fervent Catholics. Her writings had filled him with insufferably horrible boredom; they were more than merely wretched: they were wretched in every way, resembling the echoes of a tiny chapel where the solemn worshippers mumble their prayers, asking news of one another in low voices, while they repeat with a deeply mysterious air the common gossip of politics, weather forecasts and the state of the weather.

But there was even worse: a female laureate licensed by the Institute, Madame Augustus Craven, author of Recit d'une soeur, of Eliane and Fleaurange, puffed into reputation by the whole apostolic press. Never, no, never, had Des Esseintes imagined that any person could write such ridiculous nonsense. In the point of conception, these books were so absurd, and were written in such a disgusting style, that by these tokens they became almost remarkable and rare.

It was not at all among the works of women that Des Esseintes, whose soul was completely jaded and whose nature was not inclined to sentimentality, could come upon a literary retreat suited to his taste.

Yet he strove, with a diligence that no impatience could overcome, to enjoy the works of a certain girl of genius, the blue-stocking pucelle of the group, but his efforts miscarried. He did not take to the Journal and the Lettres in which Eugénie de Guérin celebrates, without discretion, the amazing talent of a brother who rhymed, with such cleverness and grace that one must go to the works of de Jouy and Écouchard Lebrun to find anything so novel and daring.

He had also unavailingly attempted to comprehend the delights of those works in which one may find such things as these:

This morning I hung on papa's bed a cross which a little girl had given him yesterday.

Or:

Mimi and I are invited by Monsieur Roquiers to attend the consecration of a bell tomorrow. This does not displease me at all.

Or wherein we find such important events as these:

On my neck I have hung a medal of the Holy Virgin which Louise had brought me, as an amulet against cholera.

Or poetry of this sort:

O the lovely moonbeam which fell on the Bible I was reading!

And, finally, such fine and penetrating observations as these:

When I see a man pass before a crucifix, lift his hat and make the sign of the Cross, I say to myself, 'There goes a Christian.'

And she continued in this fashion, without pause, until after Maurice de Guérin had died, after which his sister bewailed him in other pages, written in a watery prose strewn here and there with bits of poems whose humiliating poverty ended by moving Des Esseintes to pity.

Ah! it was hardly worth mentioning, but the Catholic party was not at all particular in the choice of its proteges and not at all artistic. Without exception, all these writers wrote in the pallid white prose of pensioners of a monastery, in a flowing movement of phrase which no astringent could counterbalance.

So Des Esseintes, horror-stricken at such insipidities, entirely forsook this literature. But neither did he find atonement for his disappointments among the modern masters of the clergy. These latter were one-sided divines or impeccably correct controversialists, but the Christian language in their orations and books had ended by becoming impersonal and congealing into a rhetoric whose every movement and pause was anticipated, in a sequence of periods constructed after a single model. And, in fact, Des Esseintes discovered that all the ecclesiastics wrote in the same manner, with a little more or a little less abandon or emphasis, and there was seldom any variations between the bodiless patterns traded by Dupanloup or Landriot, La Bouillerie or Gaume, by Dom Gueranger or Ratisbonne, by Freppel or Perraud, by Ravignan or Gratry, by Olivain or Dosithée, by Didon or Chocarne.

Des Esseintes had often pondered upon this matter. A really authentic talent, a supremely profound originality, a well-anchored conviction, he thought, was needed to animate this formal style which was too frail to support any thought that was unforseen or any thesis that was audacious.

Yet, despite all this, there were several writers whose burning eloquence fused and shaped this language, notably Lacordaire, who was one of the few really great writers the Church had produced for many years.

Immured, like his colleagues, in the narrow circle of orthodox speculations, likewise obliged to dissipate his energies in the exclusive consideration of those theories which had been expressed and consecrated by the Fathers of the Church and developed by the masters of the pulpit, he succeeded in inbuing them with novelty and in rejuvenating, almost in modifying them, by clothing them in a more personal and stimulating form. Here and there in his Conférences de Notre-Dame, were treasures of expression, audacious usages of words, accents of love, rapid movements, cries of joy and distracted effusions. Then, to his position as a brilliant and gentle monk whose ingenuity and labors had been exhausted in the impossible task of conciliating the liberal doctrines of society with the authoritarian dogmas of the Church, he added a temperament of fierce love and suave diplomatic tenderness. In his letters to young men may be found the caressing inflections of a father exhorting his sons with smiling reprimands, the well-meaning advice and the indulgent forgiveness. Some of these Des

Esseintes found charming, confessing as they did the monk's yearning for affection, while others were even imposing when they sought to sustain courage and dissipate doubts by the inimitable certainties of Faith. In fine, this sentiment of paternity, which gave his pen a delicately feminine quality, lent to his prose a characteristically individual accent discernible among all the clerical literature.

After Lacordaire, ecclesiastics and monks possessing any individuality were extremely rare. At the very most, a few pages of his pupil, the Abbé Peyreyve, merited reading. He left sympathetic biographies of his master, wrote a few loveable letters, composed treatises in the sonorous language of formal discourse, and delivered panegyrics in which the declamatory tone was too broadly stressed. Certainly the Abbé Peyreyve had neither the emotion nor the ardor of Lacordaire. He was too much a priest and too little a man. Yet, here and there in the rhetoric of his sermons, flashed interesting effects of large and solid phrasing or touches of nobility that were almost venerable.

But to find writers of prose whose works justify close study, one was obliged to seek those who had not submitted to Ordination; to the secular writers whom the interests of Catholicism engaged and devoted to its cause.

With the Comte de Falloux, the episcopal style, so stupidly handled by the prelates, recruited new strength and in a manner recovered its masculine vigor. Under his guise of moderation, this academician exuded gall. The discourse which he delivered to Parliament in 1848 was diffuse and abject, but his articles, first printed in the Correspondant and since collected into books, were mordant and discerning under the exaggerated politeness of their form. Conceived as harangues, they contained a certain strong muscular energy and were astonishing in the intolerance of their convictions.

A dangerous polemist because of his ambuscades, a shrewd logician, executing flanking movements and attacking unexpectedly, the Comte de Falloux had also written striking, penetrating pages on the death of Madame Swetchine, whose tracts he had collected and whom he revered as a saint.

But the true temperament of the writer was betrayed in the two brochures which appeared in 1848 and 1880, the latter entitled l'Unité nationale.

Moved by a cold rage, the implacable legitimist this time fought openly, contrary to his custom, and hurled against the infidels, in the form of a peroration, such fulminating invectives as these:

"And you, systematic Utopians, who make an abstraction of human nature, fomentors of atheism, fed on chimeræ and hatreds, emancipators of woman, destroyers of the family, genealogists of the simian race, you whose name was but lately an outrage, be satisfied: you shall have been the prophets, and your disciples will be the high-priests of an abominable future!"

The other brochure bore the title le Parti catholique and was directed against the despotism of the Univers and against Veuillot whose name he refused to mention. Here the sinuous attacks were resumed, venom filtered beneath each line, when the gentleman, clad in blue answered the sharp physical blows of the fighter with scornful sarcasms.

These contestants represented the two parties of the Church, the two factions whose differences were resolved into virulent hatreds. De Falloux, the more haughty and cunning, belonged to the liberal camp which already claimed Montalembert and Cochin, Lacordaire and De Broglie. He subscribed to the principles of the Correspondant, a review which attempted to cover the imperious theories of the Church with a varnish of tolerance. Veuillot, franker and more open, scorned such masks, unhesitatingly admitted the tyranny of the ultramontaine doctrines and confessed, with a certain compunction, the pitiless yoke of the Church's dogma.

For the conduct of this verbal warfare, Veuillot had made himself master of a special style, partly borrowed from La Bruyère and Du Gros-Caillou. This half-solemn, half-slang style, had the force of a tomahawk in the hands of this vehement personality. Strangely headstrong and brave, he had overwhelmed both free thinkers and bishops with this terrible weapon, charging at his enemies like a bull, regardless of the party to which they belonged. Distrusted by the Church, which would tolerate neither his contraband style nor his fortified theories, he had nevertheless overawed everybody by his powerful talent, incurring the attack of the entire press which he effectively thrashed in his Odeurs de Paris, coping with every assault, freeing himself with a kick of the foot of all the wretched hack-writers who had presumed to attack him.

Unfortunately, this undisputed talent only existed in pugilism. At peace, Veuillot was no more than a mediocre writer. His poetry and novels were pitiful. His language was vapid, when it was not engaged in a striking controversy. In repose, he changed, uttering banal litanies and mumbling childish hymns.

More formal, more constrained and more serious was the beloved apologist of the Church, Ozanam, the inquisitor of the Christian language. Although he was very difficult to understand, Des Esseintes never failed to be astonished by the insouciance of this writer, who spoke confidently of God's impenetrable designs, although he felt obliged to establish proof of the improbable assertions he advanced. With the utmost self-confidence, he deformed events, contradicted, with greater impudence even than the panegyrists of other parties, the known facts of history, averred that the Church had never concealed the esteem it had for science, called heresies impure miasmas, and treated Buddhism and other religions with such contempt that he apologized for even soiling his Catholic prose by onslaught on their doctrines.

At times, religious passion breathed a certain ardor into his oratorical language, under the ice of which seethed a violent current; in his numerous writings on Dante, on Saint Francis, on the author of Stabat Mater, on the Franciscan poets, on socialism, on commercial law and every imaginable subject, this man pleaded for the defense of the Vatican which he held indefectible, and judged causes and opinions according to their harmony or discord with those that he advanced.

This manner of viewing questions from a single viewpoint was also the method of that literary scamp, Nettement, whom some people would have made the other's rival. The latter was less bigoted than the master, affected less arrogance and admitted more worldly pretentions. He repeatedly left the literary cloister in which Ozanam had imprisoned himself, and had read secular works so as to be able to judge of them.

This province he entered gropingly, like a child in a vault, seeing nothing but shadow around him, perceiving in this gloom only the gleam of the candle which illumed the place a few paces before him.

In this gloom, uncertain of his bearings, he stumbled at every turn, speaking of Murger who had "the care of a chiselled and carefully finished style"; of Hugo who sought the noisome and unclean and to whom he dared compare De Laprade; of Paul Delacroix who scorned the rules; of Paul Delaroche and of the poet Reboul, whom he praised because of their apparent faith.

Des Esseintes could not restrain a shrug of the shoulders before these stupid opinions, covered by a borrowed prose whose already worn texture clung or became torn at each phrase.

In a different way, the works of Poujoulat and Genoude, Montalembert, Nicolas and Carné failed to inspire him with any definite interest. His taste for history was not pronounced, even when treated with the scholarly fidelity and harmonious style of the Duc de Broglie, nor was his penchant for the social and religious questions, even when broached by Henry Cochin, who revealed his true self in a letter where he gave a stirring account of the taking of the veil at the Sacré-Cœur. He had not touched these books for a long time, and the period was already remote when he had thrown with his waste paper the puerile lucubrations of the gloomy Pontmartin and the pitiful Féval; and long since he had given to his servants, for a certain vulgar usage, the short stories of Aubineau and Lasserre, in which are recorded wretched hagiographies of miracles effected by Dupont of Tours and by the Virgin.

In no way did Des Esseintes derive even a fugitive distraction from his boredom from this literature. The mass of books which he had once studied he had thrown into dim corners of his library shelves when he left the Fathers' school. "I should have left them in Paris," he told himself, as he turned out some books which were particularly insufferable: those of the Abbé Lamennais and that impervious sectarian so magisterially, so pompously dull and empty, the Comte Joseph de Maistre.

A single volume remained on a shelf, within reach of his hand. It was the Homme of Ernest Hello. This writer was the absolute opposite of his religious confederates. Almost isolated among the pious group terrified by his conduct, Ernest Hello had ended by abandoning the open road that led from earth to heaven. Probably disgusted by the dullness of the journey and the noisy mob of those pilgrims of letters who for centuries followed one after the other upon the same highway, marching in each other's steps, stopping at the same places to exchange the same commonplace remarks on religion, on the Church Fathers, on their similar beliefs, on their common masters, he had departed through the byways to wander in the gloomy glade of Pascal, where he tarried long to recover his breath before continuing on his way and going even farther in the regions of human thought than the Jansenist, whom he derided.

Tortuous and precious, doctoral and complex, Hello, by the piercing cunning of his analysis, recalled to Des Esseintes the sharp, probing investigations of some of the infidel psychologists of the preceding and present century. In him was a sort of Catholic Duranty, but more dogmatic and penetrating, an experienced manipulation of the magnifying glass, a sophisticated engineer of the soul, a skillful watchmaker of the brain, delighting to examine the mechanism of a passion and elucidate it by details of the wheel work.

In this oddly formed mind existed unsurmised relationships of thoughts, harmonies and oppositions; furthermore, he affected a wholly novel manner of action which used the etymology of words as a spring-board for ideas whose associations sometimes became tenuous, but which almost constantly remained ingenious and sparkling.

Thus, despite the awkwardness of his structure, he dissected with a singular perspicacity, the Avare, "the ordinary man," and "the passion of unhappiness," revealing meanwhile interesting comparisons which could be constructed between the operations of photography and of memory.

But such skill in handling this perfected instrument of analysis, stolen from the enemies of the Church, represented only one of the temperamental phases of this man.

Still another existed. This mind divided itself in two parts and revealed, besides the writer, the religious fanatic and Biblical prophet.

Like Hugo, whom he now and again recalled in distortions of phrases and words, Ernest Hello had delighted in imitating Saint John of Patmos. He pontificated and vaticinated from his retreat in the rue Saint-Sulpice, haranguing the reader with an apocalyptic language partaking in spots of the bitterness of an Isaiah.

He affected inordinate pretentions of profundity. There were some fawning and complacent people who pretended to consider him a great man, the reservoir of learning, the encyclopedic giant of the age. Perhaps he was a well, but one at whose bottom one often could not find a drop of water.

In his volume Paroles de Dieu, he paraphrased the Holy Scriptures, endeavoring to complicate their ordinarily obvious sense. In his other book Homme, and in his brochure le Jour du Seigneur, written in a biblical style, rugged and obscure, he sought to appear like a vengeful apostle, prideful and tormented with spleen, but showed himself a deacon touched with a mystic epilepsy, or like a talented Maistre, a surly and bitter sectarian.

But, thought Des Esseintes, this sickly shamelessness often obstructed the inventive sallies of the casuist. With more intolerance than even Ozanam, he resolutely denied all that pertained to his clan, proclaimed the most disconcerting axioms, maintained with a disconcerting authority that "geology is returning toward Moses," and that natural history, like chemistry and every contemporary science, verifies the scientific truth of the Bible. The proposition on each page was of the unique truth and the superhuman knowledge of the Church, and everywhere were interspersed more than perilous aphorisms and raging curses cast at the art of the last century.

To this strange mixture was added the love of sanctimonious delights, such as a translation of the Visions by Angèle de Foligno, a book of an unparalleled fluid stupidity, with selected works of Jean Rusbrock l'Admirable, a mystic of the thirteenth century whose prose offered an incomprehensible but alluring combination of dusky exaltations, caressing effusions, and poignant transports.

The whole attitude of this presumptuous pontiff, Hello, had leaped from a preface written for this book. He himself remarked that "extraordinary things can only be stammered," and he stammered in good truth, declaring that "the holy gloom where Rusbrock extends his eagle wings is his ocean, his prey, his glory, and for such as him the far horizons would be a too narrow garment."

However this might be, Des Esseintes felt himself intrigued toward this ill-balanced but subtile mind. No fusion had been effected between the skilful psychologist and the pious pedant, and the very jolts and incoherencies constituted the personality of the man.

With him was recruited the little group of writers who fought on the front battle line of the clerical camp. They did not belong to the regular army, but were more properly the scouts of a religion which distrusted men of such talent as Veuillot and Hello, because they did not seem sufficiently submissive and shallow. What the Church really desires is soldiers who do not reason, files of such blind combatants and such mediocrities as Hello describes with the rage of one who has submitted to their yoke. Thus it was that Catholicism had lost no time in driving away one of its partisans, an enraged pamphleteer who wrote in a style at once rare and exasperated, the savage Léon Bloy; and caused to be cast from the doors of its bookshops, as it would a plague or a filthy vagrant, another writer who had made himself hoarse with celebrating its praises, Barbey d'Aurevilly.

It is true that the latter was too prone to compromise and not sufficiently docile. Others bent their heads under rebukes and returned to the ranks; but he was the enfant terrible, and was unrecognized by the party. In a literary way, he pursued women whom he dragged into the sanctuary. Nay, even that vast disdain was invoked, with which Catholicism enshrouds talent to prevent excommunication from putting beyond the pale of the law a perplexing servant who, under pretext of honoring his masters, broke the window panes of the chapel, juggled with the holy pyxes and executed eccentric dances around the tabernacle.

Two works of Barbey d'Aurevilly specially attracted Des Esseintes, the Prêtre marié and the Diaboliques. Others, such as the Ensorcelé, the Chevalier des touches and Une Vieille Maîtresse, were certainly more comprehensive and more finely balanced, but they left Des Esseintes untouched, for he was really interested only in unhealthy works which were consumed and irritated by fever.

In these all but healthy volumes, Barbey d'Aurevilly constantly hesitated between those two pits which the Catholic religion succeeds in reconciling: mysticism and sadism.

In these two books which Des Esseintes was thumbing, Barbey had lost all prudence, given full rein to his steed, and galloped at full speed over roads to their farthest limits.

All the mysterious horror of the Middle Ages hovered over that improbable book, the Prêtre marié; magic blended with religion, black magic with prayer and, more pitiless and savage than the Devil himself, the God of Original Sin incessantly tortured the innocent Calixte, His reprobate, as once He had caused one of his angels to mark the houses of unbelievers whom he wished to slay.

Conceived by a fasting monk in the grip of delirium, these scenes were unfolded in the uneven style of a tortured soul. Unfortunately, among those disordered creatures that were like galvanized Coppelias of Hoffmann, some, like Néel de Néhou, seemed to have been imagined in moments of exhaustion following convulsions, and were discordant notes in this harmony of sombre madness, where they were as comical and ridiculous as a tiny zinc figure playing on a horn on a timepiece.

After these mystic divagations, the writer had experienced a period of calm. Then a terrible relapse followed.

This belief that man is a Buridanesque donkey, a being balanced between two forces of equal attraction which successively remain victorious and vanquished, this conviction that human life is only an uncertain combat waged between hell and heaven, this faith in two opposite beings, Satan and Christ, was fatally certain to engender such inner discords of the soul, exalted by incessant struggle, excited at once by promises and menaces, and ending by abandoning itself to whichever of the two forces persisted in the pursuit the more relentlessly.

In the Prêtre marié, Barbey d'Aurevilly sang the praises of Christ, who had prevailed against temptations; in the Diaboliques, the author succumbed to the Devil, whom he celebrated; then appeared sadism, that bastard of Catholicism, which through the centuries religion has relentlessly pursued with its exorcisms and stakes.

This condition, at once fascinating and ambiguous, can not arise in the soul of an unbeliever. It does not merely consist in sinking oneself in the excesses of the flesh, excited by outrageous blasphemies, for in such a case it would be no more than a case of satyriasis that had reached its climax. Before all, it consists in sacrilegious practice, in moral rebellion, in spiritual debauchery, in a wholly ideal aberration, and in this it is exemplarily Christian. It also is founded upon a joy tempered by fear, a joy analogous to the satisfaction of children who disobey their parents and play with forbidden things, for no reason other than that they had been forbidden to do so.

In fact, if it did not admit of sacrilege, sadism would have no reason for existence. Besides, the sacrilege proceeding from the very existence of a religion, can only be intentionally and pertinently performed by a believer, for no one would take pleasure in profaning a faith that was indifferent or unknown to him.

The power of sadism and the attraction it presents, lies entirely then in the prohibited enjoyment of transferring to Satan the praises and prayers due to God; it lies in the non-observance of Catholic precepts which one really follows unwillingly, by committing in deeper scorn of Christ, those sins which the Church has especially cursed, such as pollution of worship and carnal orgy.

In its elements, this phenomenon to which the Marquis de Sade has bequeathed his name is as old as the Church. It had reared its head in the eighteenth century, recalling, to go back no farther, by a simple phenomenon of atavism the impious practices of the Sabbath, the witches' revels of the Middle Ages.

By having consulted the Malleus maleficorum, that terrible code of Jacob Sprenger which permits the Church wholesale burnings of necromancers and sorcerers, Des Esseintes recognized in the witches' Sabbath, all the obscene practices and all the blasphemies of sadism. In addition to the unclean scenes beloved by Malin, the nights successively and lawfully consecrated to excessive sensual orgies and devoted to the bestialities of passion, he once more discovered the parody of the processions, the insults and eternal threats levelled at God and the devotion bestowed upon His rival, while amid cursing of the wine and the bread, the black mass was being celebrated on the back of a woman on all fours, whose stained bare thighs served as the altar from which the congregation received the communion from a black goblet stamped with an image of a goat.

This profusion of impure mockeries and foul shames were marked in the career of the Marquis de Sade, who garnished his terrible pleasures with outrageous sacrileges.

He cried out to the sky, invoked Lucifer, shouted his contempt of God, calling Him rogue and imbecile, spat upon the communion, endeavored to contaminate with vile ordures a Divinity who he prayed might damn him, the while he declared, to defy Him the more, that He did not exist.

Barbey d'Aurevilly approached this psychic state. If he did not presume as far as De Sade in uttering atrocious curses against the Saviour; if, more prudent or more timid, he claimed ever to honor the Church, he none the less addressed his suit to the Devil as was done in medieval times and he, too, in order to brave God, fell into demoniac nymphomania, inventing sensual monstrosities, even borrowing from bedroom philosophy a certain episode which he seasoned with new condiments when he wrote the story le Dîner d'un athée.

This extravagant book pleased Des Esseintes. He had caused to be printed, in violet ink and in a frame of cardinal purple, on a genuine parchment which the judges of the Rota had blessed, a copy of the Diaboliques, with characters whose quaint quavers and flourishes in turned up tails and claws affected a satanic form.

After certain pieces of Baudelaire that, in imitation of the clamorous songs of nocturnal revels, celebrated infernal litanies, this volume alone of all the works of contemporary apostolic literature testified to this state of mind, at once impious and devout, toward which Catholicism often thrust Des Esseintes.

With Barbey d'Aurevilly ended the line of religious writers; and in truth, that pariah belonged more, from every point of view, to secular literature than to the other with which he demanded a place that was denied him. His language was the language of disheveled romanticism, full of involved expressions, unfamiliar turns of speech, delighted with extravagant comparisons and with whip strokes and phrases which exploded, like the clangor of noisy bells, along the text. In short, d'Aurevilly was like a stallion among the geldings of the ultramontaine stables.

Des Esseintes reflected in this wise while re-reading, here and there, several passages of the book and, comparing its nervous and changing style with the fixed manner of other Church writers, he thought of the evolution of language which Darwin has so truly revealed.

Compelled to live in a secular atmosphere, raised in the heart of the romantic school, constantly being in the current of modern literature and accustomed to reading contemporary publications, Barbey d'Aurevilly had acquired a dialect which although it had sustained numerous and profound changes since the Great Age, had nevertheless renewed itself in his works.

The ecclesiastical writers, on the contrary, confined within specific limitations, restricted to ancient Church literature, knowing nothing of the literary progress of the centuries and determined if need be to blind their eyes the more surely not to see, necessarily were constrained to the use of an inflexible language, like that of the eighteenth century which descendants of the French who settled in Canada still speak and write today, without change of phrasing or words, having succeeded in preserving their original idiom by isolation in certain metropolitan centres, despite the fact that they are enveloped upon every side by English-speaking peoples.

Meanwhile the silvery sound of a clock that tolled the angelus announced breakfast time to Des Esseintes. He abandoned his books, pressed his brow and went to the dining room, saying to himself that, among all the volumes he had just arranged, the works of Barbey d'Aurevilly were the only ones whose ideas and style offered the gaminess he so loved to savor in the Latin and decadent, monastic writers of past ages.

Chapter 13

As the season advanced, the weather, far from improving, grew worse. Everything seemed to go wrong that year. After the squalls and mists, the sky was covered with a white expanse of heat, like plates of sheet iron. In two days, without transition, a torrid heat, an atmosphere of frightful heaviness, succeeded the damp cold of foggy days and the streaming of the rains. As though stirred by furious pokers, the sun showed like a kiln-hole, darting a light almost white-hot, burning one's face. A hot dust rose from the roads, scorching the dry trees, and the yellowed lawns became a deep brown. A temperature like that of a foundry hung over the dwelling of Des Esseintes.

Half naked, he opened a window and received the air like a furnace blast in his face. The dining room, to which he fled, was fiery, and the rarefied air simmered. Utterly distressed, he sat down, for the stimulation that had seized him had ended since the close of his reveries.

Like all people tormented by nervousness, heat distracted him. And his anæmia, checked by cold weather, again became pronounced, weakening his body which had been debilitated by copious perspiration.

The back of his shirt was saturated, his perinæum was damp, his feet and arms moist, his brow overflowing with sweat that ran down his cheeks. Des Esseintes reclined, annihilated, on a chair.

The sight of the meat placed on the table at that moment caused his stomach to rise. He ordered the food removed, asked for boiled eggs, and tried to swallow some bread soaked in eggs, but his stomach would have none of it. A fit of nausea overcame him. He drank a few drops of wine that pricked his stomach like points of fire. He wet his face; the perspiration, alternately warm and cold, coursed along his temples. He began to suck some pieces of ice to overcome his troubled heart—but in vain.

So weak was he that he leaned against the table. He rose, feeling the need of air, but the bread had slowly risen in his gullet and remained there. Never had he felt so distressed, so shattered, so ill at ease. To add to his discomfort, his eyes distressed him and he saw objects in double. Soon he lost his sense of distance, and his glass seemed to be a league away. He told himself that he was the play-thing of sensorial illusions and that he was incapable of reacting. He stretched out on a couch, but instantly he was cradled as by the tossing of a moving ship, and the affection of his heart increased. He rose to his feet, determined to rid himself, by means of a digestive, of the food which was choking him.

He again reached the dining room and sadly compared himself, in this cabin, to passengers seized with sea-sickness. Stumbling, he made his way to the closet, examined the mouth organ without opening any of the stops, but instead took from a high shelf a bottle of benedictine which he kept because of its form which to him seemed suggestive of thoughts that were at once gently wanton and vaguely mystic.

But at this moment he remained indifferent, gazing with lack-lustre, staring eyes at this squat, dark-green bottle which, at other times, had brought before him images of the medieval priories by its old-fashioned monkish paunch, its head and neck covered with a parchment hood, its red wax stamp quartered with three silver mitres against a field of azure and fastened at the neck, like a papal bull, with bands of lead, its label inscribed in sonorous Latin, on paper that seemed to have yellowed with age: Liquor Monachorum Benedictinorum Abbatiae Fiscannensis.

Under this thoroughly abbatial robe, signed with a cross and the ecclesiastic initials 'D.O.M.', pressed in between its parchments and ligatures, slept an exquisitely fine saffron-colored liquid. It breathed an aroma that seemed the quintessence of angelica and hyssop blended with sea-weeds and of iodines and bromes hidden in sweet essences, and it stimulated the palate with a spiritous ardor concealed under a virginal daintiness, and charmed the sense of smell by a pungency enveloped in a caress innocent and devout.

This deceit which resulted from the extraordinary disharmony between contents and container, between the liturgic form of the flask and its so feminine and modern soul, had formerly stimulated Des Esseintes to revery and, facing the bottle, he was inclined to think at great length of the monks who sold it, the Benedictines of the Abbey of Fécamp who, belonging to the brotherhood of Saint-Maur which had been celebrated for its controversial works under the rule of Saint Benoît, followed neither the observances of the white monks of Cîteaux nor of the black monks of Cluny. He could not but think of them as being like their brethren of the Middle Ages, cultivating simples, heating retorts and distilling faultless panaceas and prescriptions.

He tasted a drop of this liquor and, for a few moments, had relief. But soon the fire, which the dash of wine had lit in his bowels, revived. He threw down his napkin, returned to his study, and paced the floor. He felt as if he were under a pneumatic clock, and a numbing weakness stole from his brain through his limbs. Unable to endure it longer, he betook himself to the garden. It was the first time he had done this since his arrival at Fontenay. There he found shelter beneath a tree which radiated a circle of shadow. Seated on the lawn, he looked around with a besotted air at the square beds of vegetables planted by the servants. He gazed, but it was only at the end of an hour that he really saw them, for a greenish film floated before his eyes, permitting him only to see, as in the depths of water, flickering images of shifting tones.

But when he recovered his balance, he clearly distinguished the onions and cabbages, a garden bed of lettuce further off, and, in the distance along the hedge, a row of white lillies recumbent in the heavy air.

A smile played on his lips, for he suddenly recalled the strange comparison of old Nicandre, who likened, in the point of form, the pistils of lillies to the genital organs of a donkey; and he recalled also a passage from Albert le Grand, in which that thaumaturgist describes a strange way of discovering whether a girl is still a virgin, by means of a lettuce.

These remembrances distracted him somewhat. He examined the garden, interesting himself in the plants withered by the heat, and in the hot ground whose vapors rose into the dusty air. Then, above the hedge which separated the garden below from the embankment leading to the fort, he watched the urchins struggling and tumbling on the ground.

He was concentrating his attention upon them when another younger, sorry little specimen appeared. He had hair like seaweed covered with sand, two green bubbles beneath his nose, and disgusting lips surrounded by a dirty white frame formed by a slice of bread smeared with cheese and filled with pieces of scallions.

Des Esseintes inhaled the air. A perverse appetite seized him. This dirty slice made his mouth water. It seemed to him that his stomach, refusing all other nourishment, could digest this shocking food, and that his palate would enjoy it as though it were a feast.

He leaped up, ran to the kitchen and ordered a loaf, white cheese and green onions to be brought from the village, emphasizing his desire for a slice exactly like the one being eaten by the child. Then he returned to sit beneath the tree.

The little chaps were fighting with one another. They struggled for bits of bread which they shoved into their cheeks, meanwhile sucking their fingers. Kicks and blows rained freely, and the weakest, trampled upon, cried out.

At this sight, Des Esseintes recovered his animation. The interest he took in this fight distracted his thoughts from his illness. Contemplating the blind fury of these urchins, he thought of the cruel and abominable law of the struggle of existence; and, although these children were mean, he could not help being interested in their futures, yet could not but believe that it had been better for them had their mothers never given them birth.

In fact, all they could expect of life was rash, colic, fever, and measles in their earliest years; slaps in the face and degrading drudgeries up to thirteen years; deceptions by women, sicknesses and infidelity during manhood and, toward the last, infirmities and agonies in a poorhouse or asylum.

And the future was the same for every one, and none in his good senses could envy his neighbor. The rich had the same passions, the same anxieties, the same pains and the same illnesses, but in a different environment; the same mediocre enjoyments, whether alcoholic, literary or carnal. There was even a vague compensation in evils, a sort of justice which re-established the balance of misfortune between the classes, permitting the poor to bear physical suffering more easily, and making it difficult for the unresisting, weaker bodies of the rich to withstand it.

How vain, silly and mad it is to beget brats! And Des Esseintes thought of those ecclesiastics who had taken vows of sterility, yet were so inconsistent as to canonize Saint Vincent de Paul, because he brought vain tortures to innocent creatures.

By means of his hateful precautions, Vincent de Paul had deferred for years the death of unintelligent and insensate beings, in such a way that when they later became almost intelligent and sentient to grief, they were able to anticipate the future, to await and fear that death of whose very name they had of late been ignorant, some of them going as far to invoke it, in hatred of that sentence of life which the monk inflicted upon them by an absurd theological code.

And since this old man's death, his ideas had prevailed. Abandoned children were sheltered instead of being killed and yet their lives daily became increasingly rigorous and barren! Then, under pretext of liberty and progress, Society had discovered another means of increasing man's miseries by tearing him from his home, forcing him to don a ridiculous uniform and carry weapons, by brutalizing him in a slavery in every respect like that from which he had compassionately freed the negro, and all to enable him to slaughter his neighbor without risking the scaffold like ordinary murderers who operate single-handed, without uniforms and with weapons that are less swift and deafening.

Des Esseintes wondered if there had ever been such a time as ours. Our age invokes the causes of humanity, endeavors to perfect anæsthesia to suppress physical suffering. Yet at the same time it prepares these very stimulants to increase moral wretchedness.

Ah! if ever this useless procreation should be abolished, it were now. But here, again, the laws enacted by men like Portalis and Homais appeared strange and cruel.

In the matter of generation, Justice finds the agencies for deception to be quite natural. It is a recognized and acknowledged fact. There is scarcely a home of any station that does not confide its children to the drain pipes, or that does not employ contrivances that are freely sold, and which it would enter no person's mind to prohibit. And yet, if these subterfuges proved insufficient, if the attempt miscarried and if, to remedy matters, one had recourse to more efficacious measures, ah! then there were not prisons enough, not municipal jails enough to confine those who, in good faith, were condemned by other individuals who had that very evening, on the conjugal bed, done their utmost to avoid giving birth to children.

The deceit itself was not a crime, it seemed. The crime lay in the justification of the deceit.

What Society considered a crime was the act of killing a being endowed with life; and yet, in expelling a foetus, one destroyed an animal that was less formed and living and certainly less intelligent and more ugly than a dog or a cat, although it is permissible to strangle these creatures as soon as they are born.

It is only right to add, for the sake of fairness, thought Des Esseintes, that it is not the awkward man, who generally loses no time in disappearing, but rather the woman, the victim of his stupidity, who expiates the crime of having saved an innocent life.

Yet was it right that the world should be filled with such prejudice as to wish to repress manoeuvres so natural that primitive man, the Polynesian savage, for instance, instinctively practices them?

The servant interrupted the charitable reflections of Des Esseintes, who received the slice of bread on a plate of vermeil. Pains shot through his heart. He did not have the courage to eat this bread, for the unhealthy excitement of his stomach had ceased. A sensation of frightful decay swept upon him. He was compelled to rise. The sun turned, and slowly fell upon the place that he had lately occupied. The heat became more heavy and fierce.

"Throw this slice of bread to those children who are murdering each other on the road," he ordered his servant. "Let the weakest be crippled, be denied share in the prize, and be soundly thrashed into the bargain, as they will be when they return to their homes with torn trousers and bruised eyes. This will give them an idea of the life that awaits them!"

And he entered the house and sank into his armchair.

"But I must try to eat something," he said. And he attempted to soak a biscuit in old Constantia wine, several bottles of which remained in his cellar.

That wine, the color of slightly burned onions, partaking of Malaga and Port, but with a specially luscious flavor, and an after-taste of grapes dried by fiery suns, had often comforted him, given a new energy to his stomach weakened by the fasts which he was forced to undergo. But this cordial, usually so efficacious, now failed. Then he thought that an emollient might perhaps counteract the fiery pains which were consuming him, and he took out the Nalifka, a Russian liqueur, contained in a bottle frosted with unpolished glass. This unctuous raspberry-flavored syrup also failed. Alas! the time was far off when, enjoying good health, Des Esseintes had ridden to his house in the hot summer days in a sleigh, and there, covered with furs wrapped about his chest, forced himself to shiver, saying, as he listened attentively to the chattering of his teeth: "Ah, how biting this wind is! It is freezing!" Thus he had almost succeeded in convincing himself that it was cold.

Unfortunately, such remedies as these had failed of their purpose ever since his sickness became vital.

With all this, he was unable to make use of laudanum: instead of allaying the pain, this sedative irritated him even to the degree of depriving him of rest. At one time he had endeavored to procure visions through opium and hashish, but these two substances had led to vomitings and intense nervous disturbances. He had instantly been forced to give up the idea of taking them, and without the aid of these coarse stimulants, demand of his brain alone to transport him into the land of dreams, far, far from life.

"What a day!" he said to himself, sponging his neck, feeling every ounce of his strength dissolve in perspiration; a feverish agitation still prevented him from remaining in one spot; once more he walked up and down, trying every chair in the room in turn. Wearied of the struggle, at last he fell against his bureau and leaning mechanically against the table, without thinking of anything, he touched an astrolabe which rested on a mass of books and notes and served as a paper weight.

He had purchased this engraved and gilded copper instrument (it had come from Germany and dated from the seventeenth century) of a second-hand Paris dealer, after a visit to the Cluny Museum, where he had stood for a long while in ecstatic admiration before a marvelous astrolabe made of chiseled ivory, whose cabalistic appearance enchanted him.

This paper weight evoked many reminiscences within him. Aroused and actuated by the appearance of this trinket, his thoughts rushed from Fontenay to Paris, to the curio shop where he had purchased it, then returned to the Museum, and he mentally beheld the ivory astrolabe, while his unseeing eyes continued to gaze upon the copper astrolabe on the table.

Then he left the Museum and, without quitting the town, strolled down the streets, wandered through the rue du Sommerard and the boulevard Saint-Michel, branched off into the neighboring streets, and paused before certain shops whose quite extraordinary appearance and profusion had often attracted him.

Beginning with an astrolabe, this spiritual jaunt ended in the cafés of the Latin Quarter.

He remembered how these places were crowded in the rue Monsieur-le-Prince and at the end of the rue de Vaugirard, touching the Odeon; sometimes they followed one another like the old riddecks of the Canal-aux-Harengs, at Antwerp, each of which revealed a front, the counterpart of its neighbor.

Through the half-opened doors and the windows dimmed with colored panes or curtains, he had often seen women who walked about like geese; others, on benches, rested their elbows on the marble tables, humming, their temples resting between their hands; still others strutted and posed in front of mirrors, playing with their false hair pomaded by hair-dressers; others, again, took money from their purses and methodically sorted the different denominations in little heaps.

Most of them had heavy features, hoarse voices, flabby necks and painted eyes; and all of them, like automatons, moved simultaneously upon the same impulse, flung the same enticements with the same tone and uttered the identical queer words, the same odd inflections and the same smile.

Certain ideas associated themselves in the mind of Des Esseintes, whose reveries came to an end, now that he recalled this collection of coffee-houses and streets.

He understood the significance of those cafés which reflected the state of soul of an entire generation, and from it he discovered the synthesis of the period.

And, in fact, the symptoms were certain and obvious. The houses of prostitution disappeared, and as soon as one of them closed, a café began to operate.

This restriction of prostitution which proved profitable to clandestine loves, evidently arose from the incomprehensible illusions of men in the matter of carnal life.

Monstrous as it may appear, these haunts satisfied an ideal.

Although the utilitarian tendencies transmitted by heredity and developed by the precocious rudeness and constant brutalities of the colleges had made the youth of the day strangely crude and as strangely positive and cold, it had none the less preserved, in the back of their heads, an old blue flower, an old ideal of a vague, sour affection.

Today, when the blood clamored, youths could not bring themselves to go through the formality of entering, ending, paying and leaving; in their eyes, this was bestiality, the action of a dog attacking a bitch without much ado. Then, too, vanity fled unsatisfied from these houses where there was no semblance of resistance; there was no victory, no hoped for preference, nor even largess obtained from the tradeswoman who measured her caresses according to the price. On the contrary, the courting of a girl of the cafés stimulated all the susceptibilities of love, all the refinements of sentiment. One disputed with the others for such a girl, and those to whom she granted a rendezvous, in consideration of much money, were sincere in imagining that they had won her from a rival, and in so thinking they were the objects of honorary distinction and favor.

Yet this domesticity was as stupid, as selfish, as vile as that of houses of ill-fame. Its creatures drank without being thirsty, laughed without reason, were charmed by the caresses of a slut, quarrelled and fought for no reason whatever, despite everything. The Parisian youth had not been able to see that these girls were, from the point of plastic beauty, graceful attitudes and necessary attire, quite inferior to the women in the bawdy houses! "My God," Des Esseintes exclaimed, "what ninnies are these fellows who flutter around the cafés; for, over and above their silly illusions, they forget the danger of degraded, suspicious allurements, and they are unaware of the sums of money given for affairs priced in advance by the mistress, of the time lost in waiting for an assignation deferred so as to increase its value and cost, delays which are repeated to provide more tips for the waiters."

This imbecile sentimentality, combined with a ferociously practical sense, represented the dominant motive of the age. These very persons who would have gouged their neighbors' eyes to gain ten sous, lost all presence of mind and discrimination before suspicious looking girls in restaurants who pitilessly harassed and relentlessly fleeced them. Fathers devoted their lives to their businesses and labors, families devoured one another on the pretext of trade, only to be robbed by their sons who, in turn, allowed themselves to be fleeced by women who posed as sweethearts to obtain their money.

In all Paris, from east to west and from north to south, there existed an unbroken chain of female tricksters, a system of organized theft, and all because, instead of satisfying men at once, these women were skilled in the subterfuges of delay.

At bottom, one might say that human wisdom consisted in the protraction of all things, in saying "no" before saying "yes," for one could manage people only by trifling with them.

"Ah! if the same were but true of the stomach," sighed Des Esseintes, racked by a cramp which instantly and sharply brought back his mind, that had roved far off, to Fontenay.

Chapter 14

Several days slowly passed thanks to certain measures which succeeded in tricking the stomach, but one morning Des Esseintes could endure food no longer, and he asked himself anxiously whether his already serious weakness would not grow worse and force him to take to bed. A sudden gleam of light relieved his distress; he remembered that one of his friends, quite ill at one time, had made use of a Papin's digester to overcome his anæmia and preserve what little strength he had.

He dispatched his servant to Paris for this precious utensil, and following the directions contained in the prospectus which the manufacturer had enclosed, he himself instructed the cook how to cut the roast beef into bits, put it into the pewter pot, with a slice of leek and carrot, and screw on the cover to let it boil for four hours.

At the end of this time the meat fibres were strained. He drank a spoonful of the thick salty juice deposited at the bottom of the pot. Then he felt a warmth, like a smooth caress, descend upon him.

This nourishment relieved his pain and nausea, and even strengthened his stomach which did not refuse to accept these few drops of soup.

Thanks to this digester, his neurosis was arrested and Des Esseintes said to himself: "Well, it is so much gained; perhaps the temperature will change, the sky will throw some ashes upon this abominable sun which exhausts me, and I shall hold out without accident till the first fogs and frosts of winter."

In the torpor and listless ennui in which he was sunk, the disorder of his library, whose arrangement had never been completed, irritated him. Helpless in his armchair, he had constantly in sight the books set awry on the shelves propped against each other or lying flat on their sides, like a tumbled pack of cards. This disorder offended him the more when he contrasted it with the perfect order of his religious works, carefully placed on parade along the walls.

He tried to clear up the confusion, but after ten minutes of work, perspiration covered him; the effort weakened him. He stretched himself on a couch and rang for his servant.

Following his directions, the old man continued the task, bringing each book in turn to Des Esseintes who examined it and directed where it was to be placed.

This task did not last long, for Des Esseintes' library contained but a very limited number of contemporary, secular works.

They were drawn through his brain as bands of metal are drawn through a steel-plate from which they issue thin, light, and reduced to almost imperceptible wires; and he had ended by possessing only those books which could submit to such treatment and which were so solidly tempered as to withstand the rolling-mill of each new reading. In his desire to refine, he had restrained and almost sterilized his enjoyment, ever accentuating the irremediable conflict existing between his ideas and those of the world in which he had happened to be born. He had now reached such a pass that he could no longer discover any writings to content his secret longings. And his admiration even weaned itself from those volumes which had certainly contributed to sharpen his mind, making it so suspicious and subtle.

In art, his ideas had sprung from a simple point of view. For him schools did not exist, and only the temperament of the writer mattered, only the working of his brain interested him, regardless of the subject. Unfortunately, this verity of appreciation, worthy of Palisse, was scarcely applicable, for the simple reason that, even while desiring to be free of prejudices and passion, each person naturally goes to the works which most intimately correspond with his own temperament, and ends by relegating all others to the rear.

This work of selection had slowly acted within him; not long ago he had adored the great Balzac, but as his body weakened and his nerves became troublesome, his tastes modified and his admirations changed.

Very soon, and despite the fact that he was aware of his injustice to the amazing author of the Comédie humaine, Des Esseintes had reached a point where he no longer opened Balzac's books; their healthy spirit jarred on him. Other aspirations now stirred in him, somehow becoming undefinable.

Yet when he probed himself he understood that to attract, a work must have that character of strangeness demanded by Edgar Allen Poe; but he ventured even further on this path and called for Byzantine flora of brain and complicated deliquescences of language. He desired a troubled indecision on which he might brood until he could shape it at will to a more vague or determinate form, according to the momentary state of his soul. In short, he desired a work of art both for what it was in itself and for what it permitted him to endow it. He wished to pass by means of it into a sphere of sublimated sensation which would arouse in him new commotions whose cause he might long and vainly seek to analyze.

In short, since leaving Paris, Des Esseintes was removing himself further and further from reality, especially from the contemporary world which he held in an ever growing detestation. This hatred had inevitably reacted on his literary and artistic tastes, and he would have as little as possible to do with paintings and books whose limited subjects dealt with modern life.

Thus, losing the faculty of admiring beauty indiscriminately under whatever form it was presented, he preferred Flaubert's Tentation de saint Antoine to his Éducation sentimentale; Goncourt's Faustin to his Germinie Lacerteux; Zola's Faute de l'abbé Mouret to his Assommoir.

This point of view seemed logical to him; these works less immediate, but just as vibrant and human, enabled him to penetrate farther into the depths of the temperaments of these masters who revealed in them the most mysterious transports of their being with a more sincere abandon; and they lifted him far above this trivial life which wearied him so.

In them he entered into a perfect communion of ideas with their authors who had written them when their state of soul was analogous to his own.

In fact, when the period in which a man of talent is obliged to live is dull and stupid, the artist, though unconsciously, is haunted by a nostalgia of some past century.

Finding himself unable to harmonize, save at rare intervals, with the environment in which he lives and not discovering sufficient distraction in the pleasures of observation and analysis, in the examination of the environment and its people, he feels in himself the dawning of strange ideas. Confused desires for other lands awake and are clarified by reflection and study. Instincts, sensations and thoughts bequeathed by heredity, awake, grow fixed, assert themselves with an imperious assurance. He recalls memories of beings and things he has never really known and a time comes when he escapes from the penitentiary of his age and roves, in full liberty, into another epoch with which, through a last illusion, he seems more in harmony.

With some, it is a return to vanished ages, to extinct civilizations, to dead epochs; with others, it is an urge towards a fantastic future, to a more or less intense vision of a period about to dawn, whose image, by an effect of atavism of which he is unaware, is a reproduction of some past age.

In Flaubert this nostalgia is expressed in solemn and majestic pictures of magnificent splendors, in whose gorgeous, barbaric frames move palpitating and delicate creatures, mysterious and haughty—women gifted, in the perfection of their beauty, with souls capable of suffering and in whose depths he discerned frightful derangements, mad aspirations, grieved as they were by the haunting premonition of the dissillusionments their follies held in store.

The temperament of this great artist is fully revealed in the incomparable pages of the Tentation de saint Antoine and Salammbô where, far from our sorry life, he evokes the splendors of old Asia, the age of fervent prayer and mystic depression, of languorous passions and excesses induced by the unbearable ennui resulting from opulence and prayer.

In de Goncourt, it was the nostalgia of the preceding century, a return to the elegances of a society forever lost. The stupendous setting of seas beating against jetties, of deserts stretching under torrid skies to distant horizons, did not exist in his nostalgic work which confined itself to a boudoir, near an aulic park, scented with the voluptuous fragrance of a woman with a tired smile, a perverse little pout and unresigned, pensive eyes. The soul with which he animated his characters was not that breathed by Flaubert into his creatures, no longer the soul early thrown in revolt by the inexorable certainty that no new happiness is possible; it was a soul that had too late revolted, after the experience, against all the useless attempts to invent new spiritual liaisons and to heighten the enjoyment of lovers, which from immemorial times has always ended in satiety.

Although she lived in, and partook of the life of our time, Faustin, by her ancestral influences, was a creature of the past century whose cerebral lassitude and sensual excesses she possessed.

This book of Edmond de Goncourt was one of the volumes which Des Esseintes loved best, and the suggestion of revery which he demanded lived in this work where, under each written line, another line was etched, visible to the spirit alone, indicated by a hint which revealed passion, by a reticence permitting one to divine subtle states of soul which no idiom could express. And it was no longer Flaubert's language in its inimitable magnificence, but a morbid, perspicacious style, nervous and twisted, keen to note the impalpable impression that strikes the senses, a style expert in modulating the complicated nuances of an epoch which in itself was singularly complex. In short, it was the epithet indispensable to decrepit civilizations, no matter how old they be, which must have words with new meanings and forms, innovations in phrases and words for their complex needs.

At Rome, the dying paganism had modified its prosody and transmuted its language with Ausonius, with Claudian and Rutilius whose attentive, scrupulous, sonorous and powerful style presented, in its descriptive parts especially, reflections, hints and nuances bearing an affinity with the style of de Goncourt.

At Paris, a fact unique in literary history had been consummated. That moribund society of the eighteenth century, which possessed painters, musicians and architects imbued with its tastes and doctrines, had not been able to produce a writer who could truly depict its dying elegances, the quintessence of its joys so cruelly expiated. It had been necessary to await the arrival of de Goncourt (whose temperament was formed of memories and regrets made more poignant by the sad spectacle of the intellectual poverty and the pitiful aspirations of his own time) to resuscitate, not only in his historical works, but even more in Faustin, the very soul of that period; incarnating its nervous refinements in this actress who tortured her mind and her senses so as to savor to exhaustion the grievous revulsives of love and of art.

With Zola, the nostalgia of the far-away was different. In him was no longing for vanished ages, no aspiring toward worlds lost in the night of time. His strong and solid temperament, dazzled with the luxuriance of life, its sanguine forces and moral health, diverted him from the artificial graces and painted chloroses of the past century, as well as from the hierarchic solemnity, the brutal ferocity and misty, effeminate dreams of the old orient. When he, too, had become obsessed by this nostalgia, by this need, which is nothing less than poetry itself, of shunning the contemporary world he was studying, he had rushed into an ideal and fruitful country, had dreamed of fantastic passions of skies, of long raptures of earth, and of fecund rains of pollen falling into panting organs of flowers. He had ended in a gigantic pantheism, had created, unwittingly perhaps, with this Edenesque environment in which he placed his Adam and Eve, a marvelous Hindoo poem, singing, in a style whose broad, crude strokes had something of the bizarre brilliance of an Indian painting, the song of the flesh, of animated living matter revealing, to the human creature, by its passion for reproduction the forbidden fruits of love, its suffocations, its instinctive caresses and natural attitudes.

With Baudelaire, these three masters had most affected Des Esseintes in modern, French, secular literature. But he had read them so often, had saturated himself in them so completely, that in order to absorb them he had been compelled to lay them aside and let them remain unread on his shelves.

Even now when the servant was arranging them for him, he did not care to open them, and contented himself merely with indicating the place they were to occupy and seeing that they were properly classified and put away.

The servant brought him a new series of books. These oppressed him more. They were books toward which his taste had gradually veered, books which diverted him by their very faults from the perfection of more vigorous writers. Here, too, Des Esseintes had reached the point where he sought, among these troubled pages, only phrases which discharged a sort of electricity that made him tremble; they transmitted their fluid through a medium which at first sight seemed refractory.

Their imperfections pleased him, provided they were neither parasitic nor servile, and perhaps there was a grain of truth in his theory that the inferior and decadent writer, who is more subjective, though unfinished, distills a more irritating aperient and acid balm than the artist of the same period who is truly great. In his opinion, it was in their turbulent sketches that one perceived the exaltations of the most excitable sensibilities, the caprices of the most morbid psychological states, the most extravagant depravities of language charged, in spite of its rebelliousness, with the difficult task of containing the effervescent salts of sensations and ideas.

Thus, after the masters, he betook himself to a few writers who attracted him all the more because of the disdain in which they were held by the public incapable of understanding them.

One of them was Paul Verlaine who had begun with a volume of verse, the Poèmes Saturniens, a rather ineffectual book where imitations of Leconte de Lisle jostled with exercises in romantic rhetoric, but through which already filtered the real personality of the poet in such poems as the sonnet Rêve Familier.

In searching for his antecedents, Des Esseintes discovered, under the hesitant strokes of the sketches, a talent already deeply affected by Baudelaire, whose influence had been accentuated later on, acquiesced in by the peerless master; but the imitation was never flagrant.

And in some of his books, Bonne Chanson, Fêtes Galantes, Romances sans paroles, and his last volume, Sagesse, were poems where he himself was revealed as an original and outstanding figure.

With rhymes obtained from verb tenses, sometimes even from long adverbs preceded by a monosyllable from which they fell as from a rock into a heavy cascade of water, his verses, divided by improbable cæsuras, often became strangely obscure with their audacious ellipses and strange inaccuracies which none the less did not lack grace.

With his unrivalled ability to handle metre, he had sought to rejuvenate the fixed poetic forms. He turned the tail of the sonnet into the air, like those Japanese fish of polychrome clay which rest on stands, their heads straight down, their tails on top. Sometimes he corrupted it by using only masculine rhymes to which he seemed partial. He had often employed a bizarre form—a stanza of three lines whose middle verse was unrhymed, and a tiercet with but one rhyme, followed by a single line, an echoing refrain like "Dansons la Gigue" in Streets. He had employed other rhymes whose dim echoes are repeated in remote stanzas, like faint reverberations of a bell.

But his personality expressed itself most of all in vague and delicious confidences breathed in hushed accents, in the twilight. He alone had been able to reveal the troubled Ultima Thules of the soul; low whisperings of thoughts, avowals so haltingly and murmuringly confessed that the ear which hears them remains hesitant, passing on to the soul languors quickened by the mystery of this suggestion which is divined rather than felt. Everything characteristic of Verlaine was expressed in these adorable verses of the Fêtes Galantes:

> Le soir tombait, un soir équivoque
> d'automne,
> Les belles se pendant rêveuses à nos
> bras,
> Dirent alors des mots si spécieux tout
> bas,
> Que notre âme depuis ce temps
> tremble et s'étonne

It was no longer the immense horizon opened by the unforgettable portals of Baudelaire; it was a crevice in the moonlight, opening on a field which was more intimate and more restrained, peculiar to Verlaine who had formulated his poetic system in those lines of which Des Esseintes was so fond:

> Car nous voulons la nuance encore,
> Pas la couleur, rien que la nuance.
> Et tout le reste est litterature.

Des Esseintes had followed him with delight in his most diversified works. After his Romances sans paroles which had appeared in a journal, Verlaine had preserved a long silence, reappearing later in those charming verses, hauntingly suggestive of the gentle and cold accents of Villon, singing of the Virgin, "removed from our days of carnal thought and weary flesh." Des Esseintes often re-read Sagesse whose poems provoked him to secret reveries, a fanciful love for a Byzantine Madonna who, at a certain moment, changed into a distracted modern Cydalise so mysterious and troubling that one could not know whether she aspired toward depravities so monstrous that they became irresistible, or whether she moved in an immaculate dream where the adoration of the soul floated around her ever unavowed and ever pure.

There were other poets, too, who induced him to confide himself to them: Tristan Corbière who, in 1873, in the midst of the general apathy had issued a most eccentric volume entitled: Les Amours jaunes. Des Esseintes who, in his hatred of the banal and commonplace, would gladly have accepted the most affected folly and the most singular extravagance, spent many enjoyable hours with this work where drollery mingled with a disordered energy, and where disconcerting lines blazed out of poems so absolutely obscure as the litanies of Sommeil, that they qualified their author for the name of

Obscène confesseur des dévotes mort-nées.

The style was hardly French. The author wrote in the negro dialect, was telegraphic in form, suppressed verbs, affected a teasing phraseology, revelled in the impossible puns of a travelling salesman; then out of this jumble, laughable conceits and sly affectations emerged, and suddenly a cry of keen anguish rang out, like the snapping string of a violoncello. And with all this, in his hard rugged style, bristling with obsolescent words and unexpected neologisms, flashed perfect originalities, treasures of expression and superbly nomadic lines amputated of rhyme. Finally, over and above his Poèmes Parisiens, where Des Esseintes had discovered this profound definition of woman:

Éternel féminin de l'éternel jocrisse

Tristan Corbière had celebrated in a powerfully concise style, the Sea of Brittany, mermaids and the Pardon of Saint Anne. And he had even risen to an eloquence of hate in the insults he hurled, apropos of the Conlie camp, at the individuals whom he designated under the name of "foreigners of the Fourth of September."

The raciness of which he was so fond, which Corbière offered him in his sharp epithets, his beauties which ever remained a trifle suspect,

Des Esseintes found again in another poet, Théodore Hannon, a disciple of Baudelaire and Gautier, moved by a very unusual sense of the exquisite and the artificial.

Unlike Verlaine whose work was directly influenced by Baudelaire, especially on the psychological side, in his insidious nuances of thought and skilful quintessence of sentiment, Théodore Hannon especially descended from the master on the plastic side, by the external vision of persons and things.

His charming corruption fatally corresponded to the tendencies of Des Esseintes who, on misty or rainy days, enclosed himself in the retreat fancied by the poet and intoxicated his eyes with the rustlings of his fabrics, with the incandescence of his stones, with his exclusively material sumptuousness which ministered to cerebral reactions, and rose like a cantharides powder in a cloud of fragrant incense toward a Brussel idol with painted face and belly stained by the perfumes.

With the exception of the works of these poets and of Stéphane Mallarmé, which his servant was told to place to one side so that he might classify them separately, Des Esseintes was but slightly attracted towards the poets.

Notwithstanding the majestic form and the imposing quality of his verse which struck such a brilliant note that even the hexameters of Hugo seemed pale in comparison, Leconte de Lisle could no longer satisfy him. The antiquity so marvelously restored by Flaubert remained cold and immobile in his hands. Nothing palpitated in his verses, which lacked depth and which, most often, contained no idea. Nothing moved in those gloomy, waste poems whose impassive mythologies ended by finally leaving him cold. Too, after having long delighted in Gautier, Des Esseintes reached the point where he no longer cared for him. The admiration he felt for this man's incomparable painting had gradually dissolved; now he was more astonished than ravished by his descriptions. Objects impressed themselves upon Gautier's perceptive eyes but they went no further, they never penetrated deeper into his brain and flesh. Like a giant mirror, this writer constantly limited himself to reflecting surrounding objects with impersonal clearness. Certainly, Des Esseintes still loved the works of these two poets, as he loved rare stones and precious objects, but none of the variations of these perfect instrumentalists could hold him longer, neither being evocative of revery, neither opening for him, at least, broad roads of escape to beguile the tedium of dragging hours.

These two books left him unsatisfied. And it was the same with Hugo; the oriental and patriarchal side was too conventional and barren to detain him. And his manners, at once childish and that of a grandfather, exasperated him. He had to go to the Chansons des rues et des bois to enjoy the perfect acrobatics of his metrics. But how gladly, after all, would he not have exchanged all this tour de force for a new work by Baudelaire which might equal the others, for he, decidedly, was almost the only one whose verses, under their splendid form, contained a healing and nutritive substance. In passing from one extreme to the other, from form deprived of ideas to ideas deprived of form, Des Esseintes remained no less circumspect and cold. The psychological labyrinths of Stendhal, the analytical detours of Duranty seduced him, but their administrative, colorless and arid language, their static prose, fit at best for the wretched industry of the theatre, repelled him. Then their interesting works and their astute analyses applied to brains agitated by passions in which he was no longer interested. He was not at all concerned with general affections or points of view, with associations of common ideas, now that the reserve of his mind was more keenly developed and that he no longer admitted aught but superfine sensations and catholic or sensual torments. To enjoy a work which should combine, according to his wishes, incisive style with penetrating and feline analysis, he had to go to the master of induction, the profound and strange Edgar Allen Poe, for whom, since the time when he re-read him, his preference had never wavered.

More than any other, perhaps, he approached, by his intimate affinity, Des Esseintes' meditative cast of mind.

If Baudelaire, in the hieroglyphics of the soul, had deciphered the return of the age of sentiment and ideas, Poe, in the field of morbid psychology had more especially investigated the domain of the soul.

Under the emblematic title, The Demon of Perversity, he had been the first in literature to pry into the irresistible, unconscious impulses of the will which mental pathology now explains more scientifically. He had also been the first to divulge, if not to signal the impressive influence of fear which acts on the will like an anæsthetic, paralyzing sensibility and like the curare, stupefying the nerves. It was on the problem of the lethargy of the will, that Poe had centered his studies, analyzing the effects of this moral poison, indicating the symptoms of its progress, the troubles commencing with anxiety, continuing through anguish, ending finally in the terror which deadens the will without intelligence succumbing, though sorely disturbed. Death, which the dramatists had so much abused, he had in some manner changed and made more poignant, by introducing an algebraic and superhuman element; but in truth, it was less the real agony of the dying person which he described and more the moral agony of the survivor, haunted at the death bed by monstrous hallucinations engendered by grief and fatigue. With a frightful fascination, he dwelt on acts of terror, on the snapping of the will, coldly reasoning about them, little by little making the reader gasp, suffocated and panting before these feverish mechanically contrived nightmares.

Convulsed by hereditary neurosis, maddened by a moral St. Vitus dance, Poe's creatures lived only through their nerves; his women, the Morellas and Ligeias, possessed an immense erudition. They were steeped in the mists of German philosophy and the cabalistic mysteries of the old Orient; and all had the boyish and inert breasts of angels, all were sexless.

Baudelaire and Poe, these two men who had often been compared because of their common poetic strain and predilection for the examination of mental maladies, differed radically in the affective conceptions which held such a large place in their works; Baudelaire with his iniquitous and debased loves—cruel loves which made one think of the reprisals of an inquisition; Poe with his chaste, ærial loves, in which the senses played no part, where only the mind functioned without corresponding to organs which, if they existed, remained forever frozen and virgin. This cerebral clinic where, vivisecting in a stifling atmosphere, that spiritual surgeon became, as soon as his attention flagged, a prey to an imagination which evoked, like delicious miasmas, somnambulistic and angelic apparitions, was to Des Esseintes a source of unwearying conjecture. But now that his nervous disorders were augmented, days came when his readings broke his spirit and when, hands trembling, body alert, like the desolate Usher he was haunted by an unreasoning fear and a secret terror.

Thus he was compelled to moderate his desires, and he rarely touched these fearful elixirs, in the same way that he could no longer with impunity visit his red corridor and grow ecstatic at the sight of the gloomy Odilon Redon prints and the Jan Luyken horrors. And yet, when he felt inclined to read, all literature seemed to him dull after these terrible American imported philtres. Then he betook himself to Villiers de L'Isle Adam in whose scattered works he noted seditious observations and spasmodic vibrations, but which no longer gave one, with the exception of his Claire Lenoir, such troubling horror.

This Claire Lenoir which appeared in 1867 in the Revue des lettres et des arts, opened a series of tales comprised under the title of Histoires Moroses where against a background of obscure speculations borrowed from old Hegel, dislocated creatures stirred, Dr. Tribulat Bonhomet, solemn and childish, a Claire Lenoir, farcical and sinister, with blue spectacles, round and large as franc pieces, which covered her almost dead eyes.

This story centered about a simple adultery and ended with an inexpressible terror when Bonhomet, opening Claire's eyelids, as she lies in her death bed, and penetrating them with monstrous plummets, distinctively perceives the reflection of the husband brandishing the lover's decapitated head, while shouting a war song, like a Kanaka.

Based on this more or less just observation that the eyes of certain animals, cows for instance, preserve even to decomposition, like photographic plates, the image of the beings and things their eyes behold at the moment they expire, this story evidently derived from Poe, from whom he appropriated the terrifying and elaborate technique.

This also applied to the Intersigne, which had later been joined to the Contes cruels, a collection of indisputable talent in which was found Véra, which Des Esseintes considered a little masterpiece.

Here, the hallucination was marked with an exquisite tenderness; no longer was it the dark mirages of the American author, but the fluid, warm, almost celestial vision; it was in an identical genre, the reverse of the Beatrices and Legeias, those gloomy and dark phantoms engendered by the inexorable nightmare of opium.

This story also put in play the operations of the will, but it no longer treated of its defeats and helplessness under the effects of fear; on the contrary, it studied the exaltations of the will under the impulse of a fixed idea; it demonstrated its power which often succeeded in saturating the atmosphere and in imposing its qualities on surrounding objects.

Another book by Villiers de L'Isle Adam, Isis, seemed to him curious in other respects. The philosophic medley of Clair Lenoir was evident in this work which offered an unbelievable jumble of verbal and troubled observations, souvenirs of old melodramas, poniards and rope ladders—all the romanticism which Villiers de L'Isle Adam could never rejuvenate in his Elën and Morgane, forgotten pieces published by an obscure man, Sieur Francisque Guyon.

The heroine of this book, Marquise Tullia Fabriana, reputed to have assimilated the Chaldean science of the women of Edgar Allen Poe, and the diplomatic sagacities of Stendhal, had the enigmatic countenance of Bradamante abused by an antique Circe. These insoluble mixtures developed a fuliginous vapor across which philosophic and literary influences jostled, without being able to be regulated in the author's brain when he wrote the prolegomenæ of this work which could not have embraced less than seven volumes.

But there was another side to Villiers' temperament. It was piercing and acute in an altogether different sense—a side of forbidding pleasantry and fierce raillery. No longer was it the paradoxical mystifications of Poe, but a scoffing that had in it the lugubrious and savage comedy which Swift possessed. A series of sketches, les Demoiselles de Bienfilâtre, l'Affichage céleste, la Machine à gloire, and le Plus beau dîner du monde, betrayed a singularly inventive and keenly bantering mind. The whole order of contemporary and utilitarian ideas, the whole commercialized baseness of the age were glorified in stories whose poignant irony transported Des Esseintes.

No other French book had been written in this serious and bitter style. At the most, a tale by Charles Cros, La science de l'amour, printed long ago in the Revue du Monde-Nouveau, could astonish by reason of its chemical whims, by its affected humor and by its coldly facetious observations. But the pleasure to be extracted from the story was merely relative, since its execution was a dismal failure. The firm, colored and often original style of Villiers had disappeared to give way to a mixture scraped on the literary bench of the first-comer.

"Heavens! heavens! how few books are really worth re-reading," sighed Des Esseintes, gazing at the servant who left the stool on which he had been perched, to permit Des Esseintes to survey his books with a single glance.

Des Esseintes nodded his head. But two small books remained on the table. With a sigh, he dismissed the old man, and turned over the leaves of a volume bound in onager skin which had been glazed by a hydraulic press and speckled with silver clouds. It was held together by fly-leaves of old silk damask whose faint patterns held that charm of faded things celebrated by Mallarmé in an exquisite poem.

These pages, numbering nine, had been extracted from copies of the two first Parnassian books; it was printed on parchment paper and preceded by this title: Quelques vers de Mallarmé, designed in a surprising calligraphy in uncial letters, illuminated and relieved with gold, as in old manuscripts.

Among the eleven poems brought together in these covers, several invited him: Les fenêtres, l'épilogue and Azur; but one among them all, a fragment of the Hérodiade, held him at certain hours in a spell.

How often, beneath the lamp that threw a low light on the silent chamber, had he not felt himself haunted by this Hérodiade who, in the work of Gustave Moreau, was now plunged in gloom revealing but a dim white statue in a brazier extinguished by stones.

The darkness concealed the blood, the reflections and the golds, hid the temple's farther sides, drowned the supernumeraries of the crime enshrouded in their dead colors, and, only sparing the aquerelle whites, revealed the woman's jewels and heightened her nudity.

At such times he was forced to gaze upon her unforgotten outlines; and she lived for him, her lips articulating those bizarre and delicate lines which Mallarmé makes her utter:

O miroir!
Eau froide par l'ennui dans ton cadre

gelée
Que de fois, et pendant les heures,
  désolée
Des songes et cherchant mes souvenirs
  qui sont
Comme des feuilles sous ta glace au
  trou profond,
Je m'apparus en toi comme une ombre
  lointaine!
Mais, horreur! des soirs, dans ta
  sévère fontaine,
J'ai de mon rêve épars connu la nudité!

These lines he loved, as he loved the works of this poet who, in an age of democracy devoted to lucre, lived his solitary and literary life sheltered by his disdain from the encompassing stupidity, delighting, far from society, in the surprises of the intellect, in cerebral visions, refining on subtle ideas, grafting Byzantine delicacies upon them, perpetuating them in suggestions lightly connected by an almost imperceptible thread.

These twisted and precious ideas were bound together with an adhesive and secret language full of phrase contractions, ellipses and bold tropes.

Perceiving the remotest analogies, with a single term which by an effect of similitude at once gave the form, the perfume, the color and the quality, he described the object or being to which otherwise he would have been compelled to place numerous and different epithets so as to disengage all their facets and nuances, had he simply contented himself with indicating the technical name. Thus he succeeded in dispensing with the comparison, which formed in the reader's mind by analogy as soon as the symbol was understood. Neither was the attention of the reader diverted by the enumeration of the qualities which the juxtaposition of adjectives would have induced. Concentrating upon a single word, he produced, as for a picture, the ensemble, a unique and complete aspect.

It became a concentrated literature, an essential unity, a sublimate of art. This style was at first employed with restraint in his earlier works, but Mallarmé had boldly proclaimed it in a verse on Théophile Gautier and in l'Après-midi du faune, an eclogue where the subtleties of sensual joys are described in mysterious and caressing verses suddenly pierced by this wild, rending faun cry:

Alors m'éveillerai-je à la ferveur
première,
Droit et seul sous un flot antique de
lumière,
Lys! et l'un de vous tous pour
l'ingénuité.

That line with the monosyllable lys like a sprig, evoked the image of something rigid, slender and white; it rhymed with the substantive ingénuité, allegorically expressing, by a single term, the passion, the effervescence, the fugitive mood of a virgin faun amorously distracted by the sight of nymphs.

In this extraordinary poem, surprising and unthought of images leaped up at the end of each line, when the poet described the elations and regrets of the faun contemplating, at the edge of a fen, the tufts of reeds still preserving, in its transitory mould, the form made by the naiades who had occupied it.

Then, Des Esseintes also experienced insidious delights in touching this diminutive book whose cover of Japan vellum, as white as curdled milk, were held together by two silk bands, one of Chinese rose, the other of black.

Hidden behind the cover, the black band rejoined the rose which rested like a touch of modern Japanese paint or like a lascivious adjutant against the antique white, against the candid carnation tint of the book, and enlaced it, united its sombre color with the light color into a light rosette. It insinuated a faint warning of that regret, a vague menace of that sadness which succeeds the ended transports and the calmed excitements of the senses.

Des Esseintes placed l'Après-midi du faune on the table and examined another little book he had printed, an anthology of prose poems, a tiny chapel, placed under the invocation of Baudelaire and opening on the parvise of his poems.

This anthology comprised a selection of Gaspard de la nuit of that fantastic Aloysius Bertrand who had transferred the behavior of Leonard in prose and, with his metallic oxydes, painted little pictures whose vivid colors sparkle like those of clear enamels. To this, Des Esseintes had joined le Vox populi of Villiers, a superb piece of work in a hammered, golden style after the manner of Leconte de Lisle and of Flaubert, and some selections from that delicate livre de Jade whose exotic perfume of ginseng and of tea blends with the odorous freshness of water babbling along the book, under moonlight.

But in this collection had been gathered certain poems resurrected from defunct reviews: le Démon de l'analogie, la Pipe, le Pauvre enfant pâle, le Spectacle interrompu, le Phénomène futur, and especially Plaintes d'automne and Frisson d'hiver which were Mallarmé's masterpieces and were also celebrated among the masterpieces of prose poems, for they united such a magnificently delicate language that they cradled, like a melancholy incantation or a maddening melody, thoughts of an irresistible suggestiveness, pulsations of the soul of a sensitive person whose excited nerves vibrate with a keenness which penetrates ravishingly and induces a sadness.

Of all the forms of literature, that of the prose poem was the form Des Esseintes preferred. Handled by an alchemist of genius, it contained in its slender volume the strength of the novel whose analytic developments and descriptive redundancies it suppressed. Quite often, Des Esseintes had meditated on that disquieting problem—to write a novel concentrated in a few phrases which should contain the essence of hundreds of pages always employed to establish the setting, to sketch the characters, and to pile up observations and minute details. Then the chosen words would be so unexchangeable that they would do duty for many others, the adjective placed in such an ingenious and definite fashion that it could not be displaced, opening such perspectives that the reader could dream for whole weeks on its sense at once precise and complex, could record the present, reconstruct the past, divine the future of the souls of the characters, revealed by the gleams of this unique epithet.

Thus conceived and condensed in a page or two, the novel could become a communion of thought between a magical writer and an ideal reader, a spiritual collaboration agreed to between ten superior persons scattered throughout the universe, a delight offered to the refined, and accessible to them alone.

To Des Esseintes, the prose poem represented the concrete juice of literature, the essential oil of art.

That succulence, developed and concentrated into a drop, already existed in Baudelaire and in those poems of Mallarmé which he read with such deep joy.

When he had closed his anthology, Des Esseintes told himself that his books which had ended on this last book, would probably never have anything added to it.

In fact, the decadence of a literature, irreparably affected in its organism, enfeebled by old ideas, exhausted by excesses of syntax, sensitive only to the curiosities which make sick persons feverish, and yet intent upon expressing everything in its decline, eager to repair all the omissions of enjoyment, to bequeath the most subtle memories of grief in its death bed, was incarnate in Mallarmé, in the most perfect exquisite manner imaginable.

Here were the quintessences of Baudelaire and of Poe; here were their fine and powerful substances distilled and disengaging new flavors and intoxications.

It was the agony of the old language which, after having become moldy from age to age, ended by dissolving, by reaching that deliquescence of the Latin language which expired in the mysterious concepts and the enigmatical expressions of Saint Boniface and Saint Adhelme.

The decomposition of the French language had been effected suddenly. In the Latin language, a long transition, a distance of four hundred years existed between the spotted and superb epithet of Claudian and Rutilius and the gamy epithet of the eighth century. In the French language, no lapse of time, no succession of ages had taken place; the stained and superb style of the de Goncourts and the gamy style of Verlaine and Mallarmé jostled in Paris, living in the same period, epoch and century.

And Des Esseintes, gazing at one of the folios opened on his chapel desk, smiled at the thought that the moment would soon come when an erudite scholar would prepare for the decadence of the French language a glossary similar to that in which the savant, Du Cange, has noted the last murmurings, the last spasms, the last flashes of the Latin language dying of old age in the cloisters and sounding its death rattle.

Chapter 15

Burning at first like a rick on fire, his enthusiasm for the digester as quickly died out. Torpid at first, his nervous dyspepsia reappeared, and then this hot essence induced such an irritation in his stomach that Des Esseintes was quickly compelled to stop using it.

The malady increased in strength; peculiar symptoms attended it. After the nightmares, hallucinations of smell, pains in the eye and deep coughing which recurred with clock-like regularity, after the pounding of his heart and arteries and the cold perspiration, arose illusions of hearing, those alterations which only reveal themselves in the last period of sickness.

Attacked by a strong fever, Des Esseintes suddenly heard murmurings of water; then those sounds united into one and resembled a roaring which increased and then slowly resolved itself into a silvery bell sound.

He felt his delirious brain whirling in musical waves, engulfed in the mystic whirlwinds of his infancy. The songs learned at the Jesuits reappeared, bringing with them pictures of the school and the chapel where they had resounded, driving their hallucinations to the olfactory and visual organs, veiling them with clouds of incense and the pallid light irradiating through the stained-glass windows, under the lofty arches.

At the Fathers, the religious ceremonies had been practiced with great pomp. An excellent organist and remarkable singing director made an artistic delight of these spiritual exercises that were conducive to worship. The organist was in love with the old masters and on holidays celebrated masses by Palestrina and Orlando Lasso, psalms by Marcello, oratorios by Handel, motets by Bach; he preferred to render the sweet and facile compilations of Father Lambillotte so much favored by priests, the "Laudi Spirituali" of the sixteenth century whose sacerdotal beauty had often bewitched Des Esseintes.

But he particularly extracted ineffable pleasures while listening to the plain-chant which the organist had preserved regardless of new ideas.

That form which was now considered a decrepit and Gothic form of Christian liturgy, an archæological curiosity, a relic of ancient time, had been the voice of the early Church, the soul of the Middle Age. It was the eternal prayer that had been sung and modulated in harmony with the soul's transports, the enduring hymn uplifted for centuries to the Almighty.

That traditional melody was the only one which, with its strong unison, its solemn and massive harmonies, like freestone, was not out of place with the old basilicas, making eloquent the Romanesque vaults, whose emanation and very spirit they seemed to be.

How often had Des Esseintes not thrilled under its spell, when the "Christus factus est" of the Gregorian chant rose from the nave whose pillars seemed to tremble among the rolling clouds from censers, or when the "De Profundis" was sung, sad and mournful as a suppressed sob, poignant as a despairing invocation of humanity bewailing its mortal destiny and imploring the tender forgiveness of its Savior!

All religious music seemed profane to him compared with that magnificent chant created by the genius of the Church, anonymous as the organ whose inventor is unknown. At bottom, in the works of Jomelli and Porpora, Carissimi and Durante, in the most wonderful compositions of Handel and Bach, there was never a hint of a renunciation of public success, or the sacrifice of an effect of art, or the abdication of human pride hearkening to its own prayer.

At the most, the religious style, august and solemn, had crystallized in Lesueur's imposing masses celebrated at Saint-Roch, tending to approach the severe nudity and austere majesty of the old plain-chant.

Since then, absolutely revolted by these pretexts at Stabat Maters devised by the Pergolesis and the Rossinis, by this intrusion of profane art in liturgic art, Des Esseintes had shunned those ambiguous works tolerated by the indulgent Church.

In addition, this weakness brought about by the desire for large congregations had quickly resulted in the adoption of songs borrowed from Italian operas, of low cavatinas and indecent quadrilles played in churches converted to boudoirs and surrendered to stage actors whose voices resounded aloft, their impurity tainting the tones of the holy organ.

For years he had obstinately refused to take part in these pious entertainments, contenting himself with his memories of childhood. He even regretted having heard the Te Deum of the great masters, for he remembered that admirable plain-chant, that hymn so simple and solemn composed by some unknown saint, a Saint Ambrose or Hilary who, lacking the complicated resources of an orchestra and the musical mechanics of modern science, revealed an ardent faith, a delirious jubilation, uttered, from the soul of humanity, in the piercing and almost celestial accents of conviction.

Des Esseintes' ideas on music were in flagrant contradiction with the theories he professed regarding the other arts. In religious music, he approved only of the monastic music of the Middle Ages, that emaciated music which instinctively reacted on his nerves like certain pages of the old Christian Latin. Then (he freely confessed it) he was incapable of understanding the tricks that the contemporary masters had introduced into Catholic art. And he had not studied music with that passion which had led him towards painting and letters. He played indifferently on the piano and after many painful attempts had succeeded in reading a score, but he was ignorant of harmony, of the technique needed really to understand a nuance, to appreciate a finesse, to savor a refinement with full comprehension.

In other respects, when not read in solitude, profane music is a promiscuous art. To enjoy music, one must become part of that public which fills the theatres where, in a vile atmosphere, one perceives a loutish-looking man butchering episodes from Wagner, to the huge delight of the ignorant mob.

He had always lacked the courage to plunge in this mob-bath so as to listen to Berlioz' compositions, several fragments of which had bewitched him by their passionate exaltations and their vigorous fugues, and he was certain that there was not one single scene, not even a phrase of one of the operas of the amazing Wagner which could with impunity be detached from its whole.

The fragments, cut and served on the plate of a concert, lost all significance and remained senseless, since (like the chapters of a book, completing each other and moving to an inevitable conclusion) Wagner's melodies were necessary to sketch the characters, to incarnate their thoughts and to express their apparent or secret motives. He knew that their ingenious and persistent returns were understood only by the auditors who followed the subject from the beginning and gradually beheld the characters in relief, in a setting from which they could not be removed without dying, like branches torn from a tree.

That was why he felt that, among the vulgar herd of melomaniacs enthusing each Sunday on benches, scarcely any knew the score that was being massacred, when the ushers consented to be silent and permit the orchestra to be heard.

Granted also that intelligent patriotism forbade a French theatre to give a Wagnerian opera, the only thing left to the curious who know nothing of musical arcana and either cannot or will not betake themselves to Bayreuth, is to remain at home. And that was precisely the course of conduct he had pursued.

The more public and facile music and the independent pieces of the old operas hardly interested him; the wretched trills of Auber and Boieldieu, of Adam and Flotow and the rhetorical commonplaces of Ambroise Thomas and the Bazins disgusted him as did the superannuated affectations and vulgar graces of Italians. That was why he had resolutely broken with musical art, and during the years of his abstention, he pleasurably recalled only certain programs of chamber music when he had heard Beethoven, and especially Schumann and Schubert which had affected his nerves in the same manner as had the more intimate and troubling poems of Edgar Allen Poe.

Some of Schubert's parts for violoncello had positively left him panting, in the grip of hysteria. But it was particularly Schubert's lieders that had immeasurably excited him, causing him to experience similar sensations as after a waste of nervous fluid, or a mystic dissipation of the soul.

This music penetrated and drove back an infinity of forgotten sufferings and spleen in his heart. He was astonished at being able to contain so many dim miseries and vague griefs. This desolate music, crying from the inmost depths, terrified while charming him. Never could he repeat the "Young Girl's Lament" without a welling of tears in his eyes, for in this plaint resided something beyond a mere broken-hearted state; something in it clutched him, something like a romance ending in a gloomy landscape.

And always, when these exquisite, sad plaints returned to his lips, there was evoked for him a suburban, flinty and gloomy site where a succession of silent bent persons, harassed by life, filed past into the twilight, while, steeped in bitterness and overflowing with disgust, he felt himself solitary in this dejected landscape, struck by an inexpressibly melancholy and stubborn distress whose mysterious intensity excluded all consolation, pity and repose. Like a funeral-knell, this despairing chant haunted him, now that he was in bed, prostrated by fever and agitated by an anxiety so much the more inappeasable for the fact that he could not discover its cause. He ended by abandoning himself to the torrent of anguishes suddenly dammed by the chant of psalms slowly rising in his tortured head.

One morning, nevertheless, he felt more tranquil and requested the servant to bring a looking-glass. It fell from his hands. He hardly recognized himself. His face was a clay color, the lips bloated and dry, the tongue parched, the skin rough. His hair and beard, untended since his illness by the domestic, added to the horror of the sunken face and staring eyes burning with feverish intensity in this skeleton head that bristled with hair. More than his weakness, more than his vomitings which began with each attempt at taking nourishment, more than his emaciation, did his changed visage terrify him. He felt lost. Then, in the dejection which overcame him, a sudden energy forced him in a sitting posture. He had strength to write a letter to his Paris physician and to order the servant to depart instantly, seek and bring him back that very day.

He passed suddenly from complete depression into boundless hope. This physician was a celebrated specialist, a doctor renowned for his cures of nervous maladies "He must have cured many more dangerous cases than mine," Des Esseintes reflected. "I shall certainly be on my feet in a few days." Disenchantment succeeded his confidence. Learned and intuitive though they be, physicians know absolutely nothing of neurotic diseases, being ignorant of their origins. Like the others, this one would prescribe the eternal oxyde of zinc and quinine, bromide of potassium and valerian. He had recourse to another thought: "If these remedies have availed me little in the past, could it not be due to the fact that I have not taken the right quantities?"

In spite of everything, this expectation of being cured cheered him, but then a new fear entered. His servant might have failed to find the physician. Again he grew faint, passing instantly from the most unreasoning hopes to the most baseless fears, exaggerating the chances of a sudden recovery and his apprehensions of danger. The hours passed and the moment came when, in utter despair and convinced that the physician would not arrive, he angrily told himself that he certainly would have been saved, had he acted sooner. Then his rage against the servant and the physician whom he accused of permitting him to die, vanished, and he ended by reproaching himself for having waited so long before seeking aid, persuading himself that he would now be wholly cured had he that very last evening used the medicine.

Little by little, these alternations of hope and alarms jostling in his poor head, abated. The struggles ended by crushing him, and he relapsed into exhausted sleep interrupted by incoherent dreams, a sort of syncope pierced by awakenings in which he was barely conscious of anything. He had reached such a state where he lost all idea of desires and fears, and he was stupefied, experiencing neither astonishment or joy, when the physician suddenly arrived.

The doctor had doubtless been apprised by the servant of Des Esseintes' mode of living and of the various symptoms observed since the day when the master of the house had been found near the window, overwhelmed by the violence of perfumes. He put very few questions to the patient whom he had known for many years. He felt his pulse and attentively studied the urine where certain white spots revealed one of the determining causes of nervousness. He wrote a prescription and left without saying more than that he would soon return.

This visit comforted Des Esseintes who none the less was frightened by the taciturnity observed; he adjured his servant not to conceal the truth from him any longer. But the servant declared that the doctor had exhibited no uneasiness, and despite his suspicions, Des Esseintes could seize upon no sign that might betray a shadow of a lie on the tranquil countenance of the old man.

Then his thoughts began to obsess him less; his suffering disappeared and to the exhaustion he had felt throughout his members was grafted a certain indescribable languor. He was astonished and satisfied not to be weighted with drugs and vials, and a faint smile played on his lips when the servant brought a nourishing injection of peptone and told him he was to take it three times every twenty-four hours.

The operation succeeded and Des Esseintes could not forbear to congratulate himself on this event which in a manner crowned the existence he had created. His penchant towards the artificial had now, though involuntarily, reached the supreme goal.

Farther one could not go. The nourishment thus absorbed was the ultimate deviation one could possibly commit.

"How delicious it would be" he reflected, "to continue this simple regime in complete health! What economy of time, what a pronounced deliverance from the aversion which food gives those who lack appetite! What a complete riddance from the disgust induced by food forcibly eaten! What an energetic protestation against the vile sin of gluttony, what a positive insult hurled at old nature whose monotonous demands would thus be avoided."

And he continued, talking to himself half-aloud. One could easily stimulate desire for food by swallowing a strong aperitif. After the question, "what time is it getting to be? I am famished," one would move to the table and place the instrument on the cloth, and then, in the time it takes to say grace, one could have suppressed the tiresome and vulgar demands of the body.

Several days afterwards, the servant presented an injection whose color and odor differed from the other.

"But it is not the same at all!" Des Esseintes cried, gazing with deep feeling at the liquid poured into the apparatus. As if in a restaurant, he asked for the card, and unfolding the physician's prescription, read:

Cod Liver Oil . . . . 20 grammes
Beef Tea . . . . 200 grammes

Burgundy Wine . . . . 200 grammes

Yolk of one egg.

He remained meditative. He who by reason of the weakened state of his stomach had never seriously preoccupied himself with the art of the cuisine, was surprised to find himself thinking of combinations to please an artificial epicure. Then a strange idea crossed his brain. Perhaps the physician had imagined that the strange palate of his patient was fatigued by the taste of the peptone; perhaps he had wished, like a clever chef, to vary the taste of foods and to prevent the monotony of dishes that might lead to want of appetite. Once in the wake of these reflections, Des Esseintes sketched new recipes, preparing vegetable dinners for Fridays, using the dose of cod liver oil and wine, dismissing the beef tea as a meat food specially prohibited by the Church. But he had no occasion longer to ruminate on these nourishing drinks, for the physician succeeded gradually in curing the vomiting attacks, and he was soon swallowing, in the normal manner, a syrup of punch containing a pulverized meat whose faint aroma of cacao pleased his palate.

Weeks passed before his stomach decided to function. The nausea returned at certain moments, but these attacks were disposed of by ginger ale and Rivières' antiemetic drink.

Finally the organs were restored. Meats were digested with the aid of pepsines. Recovering strength, he was able to stand up and attempt to walk, leaning on a cane and supporting himself on the furniture. Instead of being thankful over his success, he forgot his past pains, grew irritated at the length of time needed for convalescence and reproached the doctor for not effecting a more rapid cure.

At last the day came when he could remain standing for whole afternoons. Then his study irritated him. Certain blemishes it possessed, and which habit had accustomed him to overlook, now were apparent. The colors chosen to be seen by lamp-light seemed discordant in full day. He thought of changing them and for whole hours he combined rebellious harmonies of hues, hybrid pairings of cloth and leathers.

"I am certainly on the road to recovery," he reflected, taking note of his old hobbies.

One morning, while contemplating his orange and blue walls, considering some ideal tapestries worked with stoles of the Greek Church, dreaming of Russian orphrey dalmaticas and brocaded copes flowered with Slavonic letters done in Ural stones and rows of pearls, the physician entered and, noticing the patient's eyes, questioned him.

Des Esseintes spoke of his unrealizable longings. He commenced to contrive new color schemes, to talk of harmonies and discords of tones he meant to produce, when the doctor stunned him by peremptorily announcing that these projects would never be executed here.

And, without giving him time to catch breath, he informed Des Esseintes that he had done his utmost in re-establishing the digestive functions and that now it was necessary to attack the neurosis which was by no means cured and which would necessitate years of diet and care. He added that before attempting a cure, before commencing any hydrotherapic treatment, impossible of execution at Fontenay, Des Esseintes must quit that solitude, return to Paris, and live an ordinary mode of existence by amusing himself like others.

"But the pleasures of others will not amuse me," Des Esseintes indignantly cried.

Without debating the matter, the doctor merely asserted that this radical change was, in his eyes, a question of life or death, a question of health or insanity possibly complicated in the near future by tuberculosis.

"So it is a choice between death and the hulks!" Des Esseintes exasperatedly exclaimed.

The doctor, who was imbued with all the prejudices of a man of the world, smiled and reached the door without saying a word.

Chapter 16

Des Esseintes locked himself up in his bedroom, closing his ears to the sounds of hammers on packing cases. Each stroke rent his heart, drove a sorrow into his flesh. The physician's order was being fulfilled; the fear of once more submitting to the pains he had endured, the fear of a frightful agony had acted more powerfully on Des Esseintes than the hatred of the detestable existence to which the medical order condemned him.

Yet he told himself there were people who live without conversing with anyone, absorbed far from the world in their own affairs, like recluses and trappists, and there is nothing to prove that these wretches and sages become madmen or consumptives. He had unsuccessfully cited these examples to the doctor; the latter had repeated, coldly and firmly, in a tone that admitted of no reply, that his verdict, (confirmed besides by consultation with all the experts on neurosis) was that distraction, amusement, pleasure alone might make an impression on this malady whose spiritual side eluded all remedy; and made impatient by the recriminations of his patient, he for the last time declared that he would refuse to continue treating him if he did not consent to a change of air, and live under new hygienic conditions.

Des Esseintes had instantly betaken himself to Paris, had consulted other specialists, had impartially put the case before them. All having unhesitatingly approved of the action of their colleague, he had rented an apartment in a new house, had returned to Fontenay and, white with rage, had given orders to have his trunks packed.

Sunk in his easy chair, he now ruminated upon that unyielding order which was wrecking his plans, breaking the strings of his present life and overturning his future plans. His beatitude was ended. He was compelled to abandon this sheltering haven and return at full speed into the stupidity which had once attacked him.

The physicians spoke of amusement and distraction. With whom, and with what did they wish him to distract and amuse himself?

Had he not banished himself from society? Did he know a single person whose existence would approximate his in seclusion and contemplation? Did he know a man capable of appreciating the fineness of a phrase, the subtlety of a painting, the quintessence of an idea,—a man whose soul was delicate and exquisite enough to understand Mallarmé and love Verlaine?

Where and when must he search to discover a twin spirit, a soul detached from commonplaces, blessing silence as a benefit, ingratitude as a solace, contempt as a refuge and port?

In the world where he had dwelt before his departure for Fontenay? But most of the county squires he had associated with must since have stultified themselves near card tables or ended upon the lips of women; most by this time must have married; after having enjoyed, during their life, the spoils of cads, their spouses now possessed the remains of strumpets, for, master of first-fruits, the people alone waste nothing.

"A pretty change—this custom adopted by a prudish society!" Des Esseintes reflected.

The nobility had died, the aristocracy had marched to imbecility or ordure! It was extinguished in the corruption of its descendants whose faculties grew weaker with each generation and ended in the instincts of gorillas fermented in the brains of grooms and jockeys; or rather, as with the Choiseul-Praslins, Polignacs and Chevreuses, wallowed in the mud of lawsuits which made it equal the other classes in turpitude.

The mansions themselves, the secular escutcheons, the heraldic deportment of this antique caste had disappeared. The land no longer yielding anything was put up for sale, money being needed to procure the venereal witchcraft for the besotted descendants of the old races.

The less scrupulous and stupid threw aside all sense of shame. They weltered in the mire of fraud and deceit, behaved like cheap sharpers.

This eagerness for gain, this lust for lucre had even reacted on that other class which had constantly supported itself on the nobility—the clergy. Now one perceived, in newspapers, announcements of corn cures by priests. The monasteries had changed into apothecary or liqueur workrooms. They sold recipes or manufactured products: the

Cîteaux order, chocolate; the trappists, semolina; the Maristes Brothers, biphosphate of medicinal lime and arquebuse water; the jacobins, an anti-apoplectic elixir; the disciples of Saint Benoît, benedictine; the friars of Saint Bruno, chartreuse.

Business had invaded the cloisters where, in place of antiphonaries, heavy ledgers reposed on reading-desks. Like leprosy, the avidity of the age was ravaging the Church, weighing down the monks with inventories and invoices.

And yet, in spite of everything, it was only among the ecclesiastics that Des Esseintes could hope for pleasurable contract. In the society of well-bred and learned canons, he would have been compelled to share their faith, to refrain from floating between sceptical ideas and transports of conviction which rose from time to time on the water, sustained by recollections of childhood.

He would have had to muster identical opinions and never admit (he freely did in his ardent moments) a Catholicism charged with a soupcon of magic, as under Henry the Third, and with a dash of sadism, as at the end of the last century. This special clericalism, this depraved and artistically perverse mysticism towards which he wended could not even be discussed with a priest who would not have understood them or who would have banished them with horror.

For the twentieth time, this irresolvable problem troubled him. He would have desired an end to this irresolute state in which he floundered. Now that he was pursuing a changed life, he would have liked to possess faith, to incrust it as soon as seized, to screw it into his soul, to shield it finally from all those reflections which uprooted and agitated it. But the more he desired it and the less his emptiness of spirit was evident, the more Christ's visitation receded. As his religious hunger augmented and he gazed eagerly at this faith visible but so far off that the distance terrified him, ideas pressed upon his active mind, driving back his will, rejecting, by common sense and mathematical proofs, the mysteries and dogmas. He sadly told himself that he would have to find a way to abstain from self-discussion. He would have to learn how to close his eyes and let himself be swept along by the current, forgetting those accursed discoveries which have destroyed the religious edifice, from top to bottom, since the last two centuries.

He sighed. It is neither the physiologists nor the infidels that demolish Catholicism, but the priests, whose stupid works could extirpate convictions the most steadfast.

A Dominican friar, Rouard de Card, had proved in a brochure entitled "On the Adulteration of Sacramental Substances" that most masses were not valid, because the elements used for worship had been adulterated by the manufacturers.

For years, the holy oils had been adulterated with chicken fat; wax, with burned bones; incense, with cheap resin and benzoin. But the thing that was worse was that the substances, indispensable to the holy sacrifice, the two substances without which no oblation is possible, had also been debased: the wine, by numerous dilutions and by illicit introductions of Pernambuco wood, danewort berries, alcohol and alum; the bread of the Eucharist that must be kneaded with the fine flour of wheat, by kidney beans, potash and pipe clay.

But they had gone even farther. They had dared suppress the wheat and shameless dealers were making almost all the Host with the fecula of potatoes.

Now, God refused to descend into the fecula. It was an undeniable fact and a certain one. In the second volume of his treatise on moral theology, Cardinal Gousset had dwelt at length on this question of the fraud practiced from the divine point of view. And, according to the incontestable authority of this master, one could not consecrate bread made of flour of oats, buckwheat or barley, and if the matter of using rye be less doubtful, no argument was possible in regard to the fecula which, according to the ecclesiastic expression, was in no way fit for sacramental purposes.

By means of the rapid manipulation of the fecula and the beautiful appearance presented by the unleavened breads created with this element, the shameless imposture had been so propagated that now the mystery of the transubstantiation hardly existed any longer and the priests and faithful were holding communion, without being aware of it, with neutral elements.

Ah! far off was the time when Radegonda, Queen of France, had with her own hands prepared the bread destined for the alters, or the time when, after the customs of Cluny, three priests or deacons, fasting and garbed in alb and amice, washed their faces and hands and then picked out the wheat, grain by grain, grinding it under millstone, kneading the paste in a cold and pure water and themselves baking it under a clear fire, while chanting psalms.

"All this matter of eternal dupery," Des Esseintes reflected, "is not conducive to the steadying of my already weakened faith. And how admit that omnipotence which stops at such a trifle as a pinch of fecula or a soupcon of alcohol?"

These reflections all the more threw a gloom over the view of his future life and rendered his horizon more menacing and dark.

He was lost, utterly lost. What would become of him in this Paris where he had neither family nor friends? No bond united him to the Saint-Germain quarters now in its dotage, scaling into the dust of desuetude, buried in a new society like an empty husk. And what contact could exist between him and that bourgeois class which had gradually climbed up, profiting by all the disasters to grow rich, making use of all the catastrophes to impose respect on its crimes and thefts.

After the aristocracy of birth had come the aristocracy of money. Now one saw the reign of the caliphates of commerce, the despotism of the rue du Sentier, the tyranny of trade, bringing in its train venal narrow ideas, knavish and vain instincts.

Viler and more dishonest than the nobility despoiled and the decayed clergy, the bourgeoisie borrowed their frivolous ostentations, their braggadoccio, degrading these qualities by its lack of savoir-vivre; the bourgeoisie stole their faults and converted them into hypocritical vices. And, authoritative and sly, low and cowardly, it pitilessly attacked its eternal and necessary dupe, the populace, unmuzzled and placed in ambush so as to be in readiness to assault the old castes.

It was now an acknowledged fact. Its task once terminated, the proletariat had been bled, supposedly as a measure of hygiene. The bourgeoisie, reassured, strutted about in good humor, thanks to its wealth and the contagion of its stupidity. The result of its accession to power had been the destruction of all intelligence, the negation of all honesty, the death of all art, and, in fact, the debased artists had fallen on their knees, and they eagerly kissed the dirty feet of the eminent jobbers and low satraps whose alms permitted them to live.

In painting, one now beheld a deluge of silliness; in literature, an intemperate mixture of dull style and cowardly ideas, for they had to credit the business man with honesty, the buccaneer who purchased a dot for his son and refused to pay that of his daughter, with virtue; chaste love to the Voltairian agnostic who accused the clergy of rapes and then went hypocritically and stupidly to sniff, in the obscene chambers.

It was the great American hulks transported to our continent. It was the immense, the profound, the incommensurable peasantry of the financier and the parvenu, beaming, like a pitiful sun, upon the idolatrous town which wallowed on the ground the while it uttered impure psalms before the impious tabernacle of banks.

"Well, then, society, crash to ruin! Die, aged world!" cried Des Esseintes, angered by the ignominy of the spectacle he had evoked. This cry of hate broke the nightmare that oppressed him.

"Ah!" he exclaimed, "To think that all this is not a dream, to think that I am going to return into the cowardly and servile crowd of this century!" To console himself, he recalled the comforting maxims of Schopenhauer, and repeated to himself the sad axiom of Pascal: "The soul is pained by all things it thinks upon." But the words resounded in his mind like sounds deprived of sense; his ennui disintegrated, lifting all significance from the words, all healing virtue, all effective and gentle vigor.

He came at last to perceive that the reasonings of pessimism availed little in comforting him, that impossible faith in a future life alone would pacify him.

An access of rage swept aside, like a hurricane, his attempts at resignation and indifference. He could no longer conceal the hideous truth—nothing was left, all was in ruins. The bourgeoisie were gormandizing on the solemn ruins of the Church which had become a place of rendez-vous, a mass of rubbish, soiled by petty puns and scandalous jests. Were the terrible God of Genesis and the Pale Christ of Golgotha not going to prove their existence by commanding the cataclysms of yore, by rekindling the flames that once consumed the sinful cities? Was this degradation to continue to flow and cover with its pestilence the old world planted with seeds of iniquities and shames?

The door was suddenly opened. Clean-shaved men appeared, bringing chests and carrying the furniture; then the door closed once more on the servant who was removing packages of books.

Des Esseintes sank into a chair.

"I shall be in Paris in two days. Well, all is finished. The waves of human mediocrity rise to the sky and they will engulf the refuge whose dams I open. Ah! courage leaves me, my heart breaks! O Lord, pity the Christian who doubts, the sceptic who would believe, the convict of life embarking alone in the night, under a sky no longer illumined by the consoling beacons of ancient faith."